Second Chance

LAWRENCE KEOUGH

Copyright © 2024 Lawrence Keough.

All rights reserved. No part of this book may be reproduced, stored, or transmitted by any means—whether auditory, graphic, mechanical, or electronic—without written permission of both publisher and author, except in the case of brief excerpts used in critical articles and reviews. Unauthorized reproduction of any part of this work is illegal and is punishable by law.

ISBN: 979-8-89031-685-1 (sc)
ISBN: 979-8-89031-686-8 (hc)
ISBN: 979-8-89031-687-5 (e)

Because of the dynamic nature of the Internet, any web addresses or links contained in this book may have changed since publication and may no longer be valid. The views expressed in this work are solely those of the author and do not necessarily reflect the views of the publisher, and the publisher hereby disclaims any responsibility for them.

One Galleria Blvd., Suite 1900, Metairie, LA 70001
(504) 702-6708

Acknowledgments

Acknowledge my father, Lawrence E. Keough, and posthumous recognition of both my mother, Carole R. Keough, and former English professor, Ruth Loechler, for encouraging me to hone my writing skills. Their encouragement was the impetus for me to be a journalist, speech writer and author.

Other Acknowledgements: Former Ohio representatives Marlene Anielski for passage of the Suicide Awareness & Prevention Act, and Dave Greenspan, whose legislation laid the ground work for state senators Stephanie Kunze and Theresa Gavarone to co-sponsor legislation enacted as "Collin's Law."

Contents

Chapter 1 The Fateful Act 1

Chapter 2 Pronounced Dead 10

Chapter 3 Picking up the Pieces 17

Chapter 4 A New Beginning 23

Chapter 5 Trey's Recovery 29

Chapter 6 Trey's Childhood Misery 34

Chapter 7 Bad to Worse 44

Chapter 8 Straw that Broke the Camel's Back 72

Chapter 9 Trey's Planned Demise 86

Chapter 10 Risky Business 91

Chapter 11 De Ja Vu 104

Chapter 12 Perception or Reality 115

Chapter 13 The Verdict 124

Chapter 14 Trey on the Prowl 133

Chapter 15 Primrose Path 142

Chapter 16 A Brighter Future 153

Epilogue 165

Chapter 1

The Fateful Act

Trey Barry was the lone motorist on the center span of the Skyway Bridge on a late March evening in 2019 as swirling winds ruffled the Bay waters below. He lifted the handbrake in his Volkswagen Beetle, turned the ignition off, pausing as he contemplated the finality of what he was about to do.

Appearing calmly deliberative, having mentally rehearsed the steps for this anticipated fateful night, Trey depressed the hazard button and surveyed the dashboard to ensure headlights and taillights were illuminated for other motorists to avoid a collision with his parked car on the iconic bridge between St. Petersburg and Bradenton. He breathed inward, then audibly exhaled as if were on the brink of the abyss.

Trey's moment of fate had arrived after enduring what seemed like unending penance for living a pacifist's blighted journey. He exited the car and did not look back. He took a few short steps with purpose and obedience to a self-induced script, ascending atop the center span.

His oval shaped green eyes fixated on the sea water 180 feet below as his collar- length blond hair tousled in the blustery wind. A full moon displayed the froth from the cresting white caps in the choppy waters. Stepping over the rail of the center span, he was on the cusp of the unthinkable.

The metaphorical dye had been cast. There would be no turning back as he refused to engage in contemplative ambivalence. His decision was emboldened by an excruciatingly painful and indelible memory of his tormenting life over 21 plus years, rife with recurring insatiable bullying and mortified public shaming.

Trey recollected his dark interpretation of an otherwise heartfelt embrace of a poetic verse: "Life is not measured by the number of breaths we take, but by the moments that take our breath away."

For Trey, the breaths that had been taken away were neither from a glorious sun setting over the ocean, nor the pristine sights and sounds of spring water cascading hundreds of feet below onto a rock bed. Rather, his breathlessness was borne from audacious-subversive acts perpetrated upon him for predators' hedonistic enjoyment.

Trey was not bullied for being a 90-pound weakling. He was a physical specimen with an athletic build at 6-feet tall and a solid 190 pounds. A compulsive weight lifter, he had broad shoulders, bulging biceps and an overall chiseled physique. And with a thin waist line and small hips, he possessed a unique combination of brawn and sprinter speed.

But aside from his physique, he was reputed as a Teddy Bear and spineless capitulator.

Those who casually knew Trey considered him to be his own worst enemy, citing his naivete and sanguine approach as his Achilles' heel. He was misunderstood for not presenting an outward bravado and a non-verbal vibe of confidence and willingness to stand his ground to fight the good fight.

Trey was accused of lacking the intuitive senses and pragmatism to understand most bullies were cowards who preyed on the weak. He could be mistaken for a masochist for refusing evasive tactics. He was transparent and predictable to a fault, refusing to retract his head in a proverbial turtle shell for protection.

But much like a misunderstood profit, Trey's pacifism was not affirmed in the Godless society in which he lived. There were few, if any attempts for anyone outside of his inner circle to understand he was defined by this Catholic faith.

While embracing Gospel Values of respect and dignity for all God's people, he was perceived as emasculated and as such, lacking masculinity to be a man's man.

There were accusations he had no strategy to combat exploitation, leaving him ill-prepared for the sobering reality he was at the mercy of his attackers.

At times, he arbitrarily embraced his victimization as if it were a cross to bear, accepting it as his way of life. On other occasions, he attempted to ignore bullies in a false reality as if they did not exist.

This provided fodder that what he ignored is empowered and silence is a form of complicity for failing to hold those accountable for mendacity and exploitation upon him.

Trey's distractors contended that if he had embraced strength in numbers by reaching out to his parents and siblings for support, bullies may have thought twice about targeting him.

But if Trey refused to build an inner sanctum of support, he was not alone. His situation was not dramatically different than women who remain in abusive relationships, repeatedly victims of domestic violence, nary saying a word.

Trey's refusal to defend himself against bullies was not from cowardice and timidity, but a sincere conviction fighting was not the answer. As the consummate pacifist, Trey had neither pugnaciousness, nor hutzpah. He literally turned the other cheek in refusing to defend himself.

Moreover, he did not distinguish self-defense from fighting. In his mind. it was all the same. Trey marched to the tune of his own drummer, walking the straight and narrow in his Catholic faith.

Trey's principles, based on conscience, distinguished right from wrong, morality from immorality and fairness and unfairness, required him to be the voice for the least of his brothers and sisters in Christ. He embraced corporal works of mercy as the student with the fortitude to voice an unpopular viewpoint in class if he believed it to be meritorious. He also was the one who befriended classmates who were alone.

Trey had grace and serene countenance to tip his proverbial hat to an adversary. Trey realized he could not control the behavior of others but refused to expediently modify his actions in order to ingratiate himself to those who posed a threat to him.

To do otherwise, would have violated his conscience.

For Trey, lying and manipulation were unacceptable, even if they were the means for him to avoid public pummeling. He would not portend to be someone he is not.

Paradoxically, his refusal to engage in fisticuffs was laudable, yet made him the easiest of targets. Bullies knew they could beat and shame him without retribution.

But he had an abiding and resolute faith that although people may abandon him, God the Father and his only begotten Son always will be with him.

To that end, the biblical verse in Mark, Ch. 4, 35-41 reaffirmed this belief in which Jesus and the Apostles were in a boat as a treacherous storm descended upon them. The Apostles awakened Jesus, who had been asleep in the aft of the boat, and said, "Teacher, do you not care that we are perishing?"

Jesus responded by rebuking the wind and said to the sea: "Peace! Be still."

And then there were calm seas.

Trey also listened to music for solace. Don McLean's song, "Starry, Starry Night," particularly resonated with him in which renowned artist Vincent Van Gogh no longer had the will to endure the wretchedness of this world and committed suicide.

In the days leading up to Trey's decision to end his life, he compulsively listened to a verse in the song about Van Gogh and his tragic life:

"But I told you, Vincent, this world was never meant for one as beautiful as you."

Trey did not embrace self-adulation, but he could relate to that verse, believing this world was not meant for him.

Trey turned his attention to the Gulf waters below him. "No one will ever hurt me again," he told himself while peering into the dark of night. He had an abiding-unequivocal sense he was right to end his life, forgetting the countless times his decision-making betrayed him.

Trey assumed his parents, Thomas and Katharine, would be righteously indignant with his decision to commit suicide. However, it was almost as if he secretly plied them for not understanding his life had become excruciatingly unbearable.

Trey was acutely aware of the moment. He was temporal, embracing the here and now in the spirit of carpe diem as he felt the chilled air, surveyed the lunar illumination of the night and heard the annoying cawing of seagulls circling over fishermen at the Skyway pier, a section of the old Skyway Bridge no longer operable for traffic.

A new bridge was built for north and south bound lanes after a freighter crashed into the old Skyway, damaging it beyond repair in 1980.

Trey was stoic and at peace. In many respects, this was the easy way out, to end all suffering as he knew it. He looked beyond the Gulf waters, gazing at a beacon. The Egmont Key Lighthouse immediately was within his sights, which was several miles west of the Skyway. He paused, remembering nostalgic thoughts about boating at Egmont Key when he was a young boy. But those memories were like placing a band aid on an open wound. There simply were not enough of the good times to offset the misery, which was indelibly seared in the recesses of his mind.

Ugly thoughts flashed through his mind, prompting him to wonder why so many parents abdicate their responsibility by failing to teach their children to live by the Golden Rule and Gospel Values. Trey had righteous fury about parents aiding and abetting their children to be empathy-less in which common decency and civility gave way to a me-first minded sociopathic behavior. He had observed on more occasions than he cared to remember parents accentuating friendship over discipline in rearing their children. This explained in part why parents supported and defended egregious behavior from their children, accentuating permissiveness over tough love.

Trey had seen parents justify their children's vulgarities, pulling hair, biting, kicking and other subversive acts. He was sickened by parental interference and influence empowering privileged kids to bully and ostracize weaker and vulnerable children without any expiation.

Trey was convinced this parental behavior should have been met with anathema.

But it wasn't.

In Trey's mind, malevolence among America's youth was more of the norm than the exception. And, it was an existential threat to families, communities, American culture and our nation's collective conscience to prioritize life.

If only other parents were more like his mother and father, who taught their children to treat others like they wanted to be treated. Trey recollected his parents telling him as he began kindergarten to obey his teacher as if she were his mother away from home.

Trey told himself far too many people practice idolatry and endemic permissiveness in which privilege and impunity were their gods. He still had the psychological scars from not belonging as a then fragile second grade student. The mother of a classmate had delivered invitations to the teacher for her son's birthday party as a non-school activity.

The teacher, Miss Carla Pennington, assumed there were invitations for each student. But there was no invitation for Trey. The mother's son did not want Trey to attend his birthday party. Instead of having a teaching moment with her son, the mother excused his extrication of Trey.

Trey learned at an early age life is not fair. Even as an elementary school student, he had a sense of hopelessness that the wrongs against him would not be righted.

Young Trey was a loner. When he returned home from grade school each day, he sought solace from the Barrys' family pet, Penny, the runt of a litter as part Boxer and Labrador Retriever. The tag on Penny's collar stated: "A dog does not have to be a pedigree to be a best friend." Penny was indeed Trey's best friend.

When Trey entered the Barry home, Penny ran in figure eights with euphoria they once again were united. Penny followed Trey to the kitchen, where he picked up cookies and dog biscuits. They invariably transitioned to the back yard in which Trey spewed his pent-up frustrations to his K-9 confidant.

Penny usually starred at Trey while occasionally chewing biscuits as if she understood his trials and tribulations.

As a kindergarten student, Trey was much like many of his classmates who possessed a children's innocence about the world around them. Through Trey's young eyes, everyone was a potential friend. He was both magnanimous and pollyana in which he excused rude and obnoxious behavior as an aberration. His naivety shrouded him from understanding the definition of insanity: doing the same thing over while expecting a different result.

But by sixth grade, most of Trey's classmates were hardened, embracing a mentality of survival of the fittest. They understood aggressors got what they wanted. For the very few who resisted aggression, they were at the mercy of the ring leaders and their minions. Each day was a living hell for them as they were taunted, teased, and forced to relinquish their lunches or lunch money.

If there were an unofficial code within the school, it should have been: "Prey on your classmates or be preyed upon." And so it was, most students went on the attack to avoid being attacked.

Each incident of exploitation was akin to a trophy. Students who accumulated an impressive list of trophies were protected by the ring leaders of the school. And, there was no recourse, as teachers turned a blind eye and deaf ear to what they conveniently deemed "tattle tailing."

The shame of it was adults were unwilling to protect defenseless children, who might as well have had "victim" written across their foreheads.

But self-preservation and poor parenting did not fully explain bullying. In Trey's mind, some people are psychologically flawed. As a dilettante of sorts practicing psychological theory without a license, he applied lessons from a rudimentary psychology course featuring Sigmund Freud's structure of internal conflict within the mind: the ID – desires of pleasure – is at odds with both the superego – morality and being a good person – and ego – state of consciousness.

Trey was convinced most bullies had a weak ego and superego that allowed their ID to control their aggressive personalities.

Trey secretly wished he had been born in a different time and place when boys were raised to be gentlemen and girls reared as ladies. In this pensive moment, he peered upward as if he were searching for answers from heaven. His arms were stretched outward as he appeared to be asking for divine inspiration why love is bastardized in our popular culture.

"One of the most misused words in the lexicon is love," Trey told himself. The lines on his face were strewn with anguish as he recollected why love is associated with so many behaviors, from trite or superficial romance, seductiveness and dalliance, to authenticated lasting love. He embraced the latter within the context of wedding vows, "to love for better or worse, for sickness or in health until death do us part."

Trey had a fluid understanding of the real definition of love, which was steeped in the ancient Greek term "agape." His Catholic faith had taught him the definition of agape was applied in the New Testament; John, Ch. 12, verses 34-35 in which Jesus stated: "A new command I give you, love one another as I have loved you, so you must love one another.

"By this, everyone will know you are my disciples, if you love one another."

As a devout Catholic, Trey was well aware of Mother Teresa expounding upon that verse when she wrote: "Love demands sacrifice. But if we love until it hurts, God will give us his peace and joy."

Trey was initially confused, assuming love and hurt are contradictory. But he subsequently understood the paradox when his former religious education teacher, Mary Danaher, explained as most parents understand, selfless, unconditional love is to suffer for others.

For Trey, the definition of love was crystalized when Pope Francis explained to love like Christ means saying "no" to other loves that the world offers us, such as the love of success, vanity, money and power.

"These are deceptive paths", the pontiff said, "that distance us from the Lord's love and lead us to become more and more selfish, narcissistic and overbearing."

Trey, somewhat mesmerized from his reflection on love, mumbled in soliloquy: "Love bares all and ends all." These thoughts were yet another reminder why Trey had disdain for living. It was in his most morose thoughts he convinced himself the death knell for human decency is refusing to care about the common good for all humanity.

The enormity of it all was too much for him to bear. With that thought, Trey gestured in the name of the Father, Son and Holy Spirit. He was ready to take the leap, to be the 639th person to jump from the Sunshine SkywayBridge since the original bridge was constructed in 1954. He then freed his hands from the rail of the bridge, placed his weight on his toes and lithely sprung outwardly.

Chapter 2

Pronounced Dead

It was almost surreal. Trey felt as if his body were suspended in air. But a split second later, he recollected voices of his parents and suddenly had ambivalent thoughts. He wanted a do over as he clung to his existential life while free falling.

Trey was not aware his mea culpa was typical of young people attempting suicide. Despite his misgivings, his descent would seem to suggest an irreversible certain death. Trey instinctively braced for impact and his demise. The utter shock of his body crashing into the water momentarily reduced him to a catatonic state, quivering sporadically.

Almost instantaneously, Trey was imbibed with salt water, filling his lungs as if they would burst through his chest while cracked ribs exacerbated his breathing. Trey was no longer in control. His seemingly lifeless body was at the mercy of the law of physics. He rolled head over heels, descending fathoms below the surface.

Instead of fulfilling his previous death wish, his teeth gnashed while his lips refused to part. If he were to drown, it would not be without a fight to live.

Once his downward spiral abated, Trey was in a moribund state, literally fighting for his next breath. His body was in survival mode with his brain triggering a surge of adrenaline inducing his heart into overdrive and infusing blood into major muscle groups.

Trey no longer was in a paralytic state of tonic immobility. In an indefatigable effort to avoid drowning, his legs frantically propelled him to the surface. When his head emerged above the surface, he instantaneously exhaled, then gasped for air. His head throbbed with mind numbing pain—a sure sign he was in a severely concussed state.

But the head trauma had in effect dulled the very real pain of his bruised and battered body

In his discombobulated state, Trey suddenly was blinded by a bright light. He immediately thought he was within the swath of the beckon from Egmont Key. In reality, lighthouses are landmarks for captains of vessels to see, not for beckons to shine light on specific objects. Moreover, Trey still was in close proximity to the Skyway Bridge and miles from Egmont Key.

As Trey attempted to focus from blurry-eyed vision, he heard voices, vociferously calling for him to grab a life jacket attached to a line. He was not sure whether he was hallucinating or actually hearing voices.

Regardless of whether the voices were reality, Trey's injured body was in no position to swim an inexhaustible 75 feet in gusty winds and 3-4-foot seas to reach the life jacket. For a few short moments, there was an eerily silence. He no longer heard voices, whether they were in his head or real.

Trey heard a sporadic splash over choppy waves and small craft warning-like winds. Trey feared the splash came from a large predator fish, possibly a shark. Fishermen were reputed for chumming the waters around the Skyway, attracting Hammerhead and Lemon sharks.

Trey was raised in south St. Petersburg a few blocks from the Pinellas Bayway. He enjoyed boating but was petrified of sharks. As a young boy, Trey saw firsthand the mere presence of sharks in bay area waters forcing all other marine life to skedaddle. Like many millennials, he had seen the Jaws movie and sequels.

But those were fictional movies. What frightened Trey to his core were boyhood memories of fishermen catching a 13-foot Hammerhead in Bunces Pass, a proverbial stone's throw from the Skyway. He never forgot the shark was the same size as his family's boat, ironically manufactured by North Carolina-based Hammerhead Boats Inc. Trey's aversion to sharks begged the question why he chose these very same waters for his attempted suicide.

The answer to that question essentially was the lesser of two evils. Trey did not want his parents or siblings to find him dead. It was a safe bet if anyone found his body in the Gulf or Bay waters, it would not be his immediate family.

Aside from his aversion to sharks, Trey was most content on a boat, at the beach, or at O'Neill's Marina near Maximo Park in South St. Petersburg.

This was his escape – to gawk at the moored vessels, buy a bottle of ice tea and a dozen shrimp in the bait shop and fish on a nearby dock. It was his utopia as he was extricated from people in a stress-free environment with a fishing pole in one hand and beverage in the other.

The idyllic times from fishing reminded Trey of an inscription on a dock: "There is a certain charm of fishing that comes with pursuing both the elusiveness and attainability of the catch in which there is a perpetual series of occasions for hope."

Even at a young age, Trey had "sea legs' to lithely maneuver around nautical cleats and lines strewn on floating docks. His prowess for boating carried over to the classroom, where he passed the Power Squadron's Seamanship course with flying colors as a then 12-year-old.

It was from that course Trey learned to tie an assortment of nautical knots, from the bow line, to the cleat knot, clove hitch and square knot. He even learned the time-tested art of splicing lines by infusing them together, a skill common among sailors of yesteryear.

If Trey were to be remembered for anything other than his hellish journey as a pacifist, it might be his eclectic base of maritime prowess.

When a tender was within ready reach, he realized, even in his confused state, the sound of the splash was a small boat pitching in the rolling waves and the light he presumed to be from a lighthouse was a Q-Beam on the boat.

Within moments, a young man, Jake Vanderweid, kneeling next to the port gunwale of the tender, extended his hand to Trey, who was unable to lift his arm. Jake jumped in the water and pulled Trey to the bow of the diminutive vessel.

A middle-age man, Zack Cook, inside the tender, grabbed Trey under his arms, and together, he and Jake lifted Trey's body inside the boat. A groggy Trey overheard Zack and Jake asking one another why anyone would jump from the Skyway.

"What a crazy jackass thing to do, jumping from the Skyway," Jake opined. "Hopefully, this one gets a second chance to live."

The tender made its way to its mother ship, a 52-foot, 28-ton trawler. The captain, Raphael Garza, had contacted the Coast Guard, communicating his GPS coordinates. A Coast Guard rescue boat, moored at O' Neill's Marina, was immediately summoned. Trey wrapped in a blanket and reposed on an aft bench, could see through his squinting salt water-wrenched eyes a respectful-leering gaze from Captain Garza.

Trey made eye contact with the Captain, who momentarily left the helm station to make way to the aft deck. Captain Garza leaned over Trey and shook his head in disbelief, then spoke: "You are lucky to be alive young man." Those who jump usually do not make it."

Trey did not feel lucky. He was in a state of fragility both mentally and physically. His sunken-sullen eyes foretold a morose dejection as he clung to life. In Trey's mind-numbing state, he was distancing himself from his former self who was convinced an hour ago his life was not worth living.

But now Trey inexplicably had a newfound will to live. This realization was reminiscent of a distraught man who sustained a self-inflicted gunshot to his head and amazingly lived. And even more amazing, the man who wanted to die before much of his head and face were destroyed wanted a second chance.

As Captain Garza pivoted to tend to his duties, he stopped and told Trey a rescue boat would arrive in a few minutes. Trey's collapsed lung impeded his breathing, making it impossible for him to talk. He simply nodded at the captain to express gratitude.

Trey then looked upward to the heavens, asking no one in particular how he was in this God forsaken nightmare, as if he had instantly incurred a case of amnesia. Within 20 minutes, the rescue boat arrived at the trawler. He was transferred to the other vessel, which returned to O'Neill's Marina to an awaiting ambulance.

Trey was rushed to St. Petersburg General Hospital. His seemingly short life had come full circle. The hospital was where Trey had come into the world on Nov. 6, 1997. Arriving at the hospital, he was wheeled on a stretcher to intensive care as his blood pressure dropped to fatal levels. He was in and out of consciousness as his body was shutting down with two collapsed lungs, head trauma, contusions, and considerable internal bleeding.

As Trey's placid and limp body was reposed on a gurney within the Intensive Care Unit, his next breath could be his last. His body was becoming numb to excruciating pain, a sign death was upon him.

There would be no last-word anthologies. Trey was incapable of eloquent and enunciated linguistic patterns in a fully conscious state, but in his moribund decline, his lips moved with an audible utterance with nonsensical dribble.

And then Trey, named after his Irish born great grandfather who came to America with little more than the clothes on his back, was prescribed clinically dead 20 minutes later at 1:59 am.

There was great irony and contrast in the two men who shared the same name. The great grandfather, who ascended to president and general manager of a high-end department-store, forever sealed his legacy as a self-made man.

Trey and his great grandfather had much in common.

Both men had strong resolve and intestinal fortitude to do right by living life on their terms.

But unlike his great grandfather, Trey was an easy mark for victimization.

As early as Trey's preschool years, there were premonitions Trey would be a loner. He rarely cried, had ACID reflux and stayed to himself, primarily because he was ostracized by other children.

Trey nearly always was dubbed "it" when playing hide n' seek with other kids.

Trey, even at a young age, intentionally refused to take on the combative nature of the doggy-dog world within secular society. And, in doing so, he refused to embrace the credo – without struggle, there is no progress.

He undeniably had resolve to be an eternal optimist while merciful at his core. This, however, impeded him from neither relating, nor understanding the make-up of a bully.

Spiritually, he was right to be merciful and refrain from responding to an evil act such as bullying. His Catholic faith had taught him to shun evil within the context of the famous biblical verse -- "But I tell you, do not resist an evil person. If anyone slaps you on the right check, turn to them the other cheek also. And if anyone wants to sue you and take your shirt, hand over your coat as well."

But just as the Catholic Church encourages abused women to leave their abusers, it would have exhorted Trey to do the same.

Moments after Trey was clinically dead, he was in a state of after-life. In an out-of-body experience, Trey saw himself in a narrow gothic-looking tunnel. Adorning the walls of the tunnel were ostentatiously-looking figure heads, emblematic of a demonic decor. Trey felt as if he were in a nightmare.

But was he? The tunnel seemed so real as if the montage of art had mordantly transformed into serpent-like creatures. Moreover, was the tunnel a precursor for a foreboding afterlife because he impeded God's plan for him by jumping from the Skyway Bridge?

As Trey proceeded through the tunnel, there was no light, except for what looked like a conflagration in the distance. Could he be on an inescapable journey to the fires of hell, or was this pure sophistry?

And then in that moment, the hellish odyssey ended. Trey had literally returned from the dead. This was Trey's seismic moment to have been clinically dead and then revived.

Chapter 3

Picking up the Pieces

Trey wondered if his gauntly-looking eyes were betraying him when he saw his parents and an old family friend, Fr. Liam O'Malley. When Thomas and Katharine had heard what all parents fear most—their child may die—they did not hesitate to beckon Fr. Liam.

Fr. Liam, in close proximity to the hospital as pastor of St. Mary Catholic Church, located in downtown St. Petersburg where the Barry children made their Catechetical sacraments - Baptism, First Holy Communion, Reconciliation and Confirmation.

As Trey was on the brink of death, Thomas and Katharine wanted their son to be anointed of the sick and absolved of sins through confession in the Catholic tradition of Last Rites and bestowed with the initial administration of the Eucharist known as Viaticum, the Latin term for "with you on the way."

Fr. Liam was much more than the Barrys' parish priest. He and Thomas became best friends when they were football teammates at St. Petersburg Catholic High School in the mid 1970s. Liam had been the quarterback of the varsity football team. Thomas, the punter and placekicker, teased Liam that his passes seldom hit the ground because they were either caught by his teammates or intercepted by opponents.

Thomas had wanted to be one of Liam's offensive teammates. But at 5-foot, six inches tall and a paltry 110 pounds, he was too small. But Thomas thrived as the team's place kicker. It just so happened Thomas had a personal coach. Fr. Brendan O'Reilly, a visiting priest from Ireland. He had prowess for kicking a football, given his stardom as the rugby player in his native country.

On a good day, Fr. O'Reilly could stand at the 50-yard line, turn to one end zone and boot a football between the goal posts and then turn to the other end zone and do the same. It was a spectacle to behold.

Under Fr. O'Reilly's tutelage, Thomas was the gold standard to kick field goals once the offense was stymied in the red zone. Other than place kicking, Fr. O'Reilly did not know much about American football. But he knew the defense's objective was to "kill the quarterback."

Fr. O'Reilly, also the team's chaplain, stood on the sideline during games and bellowed in his thick Irish rogue, "Kill the Quarterback." It did not seem to matter whether St. Petersburg Catholic was on offense or defense. Fr. O'Reilly could be heard encouraging all comers to amp up their efforts to attack any quarterback, Liam or otherwise.

Initially, Fr. O'Reilly well intentioned gaffe was embraced with humor. However, eventually, his oft repeated refrain wore on Liam, prompting him to ask Thomas to have a talk with Fr. O'Reilly.

To this day, Thomas is adamant he had the talk. Regardless, it appeared to be an exercise in futility because Fr. O'Reilly was not persuaded to discontinue his chant.

Thomas' lack of size did little to alleviate his regret for not being a "real» player," especially when Liam told him at their 10-year high-school reunion that among his fondest memories in life was the brotherhood he felt among his teammates. Thomas remembered Liam telling him, "I will not forget the blood, sweat and tears and knowing each of us had had one another's back and no one was above the team."

Fr. Liam and Thomas had the uncanny ability to recall highlights of games from yesteryear. Those conversations were wearing on anyone within earshot. On one such occasion, Katharine interrupted her husband in mid-sentence, declaring," You guys can remember some God forsaken game decades ago, but you can't recall what happened last week."

Katharine's sardonic assertion prompted Thomas to respond: "Don't be too harsh on us, dear. You know my long-term memory is great; my short-term memory is not so good."

They graduated in the class of 1976, which featured Liam as Val Victorian. Before parting company to head off to college, Liam and Thomas listened to America's biggest-selling records while enjoying the sun and sea at St. Pete Beach between the Don Caesar and Bonaire hotels.

This was what they did without exception throughout high school: listen to Casey Kasem's top 40 countdown of the 1970s genre of popular music. It made perfect sense when they bid farewell, to quote Kasem's famous signature line as host of the countdown: "Keep your feet on the ground and keep reaching for the stars."

In the next journeys of their lives, Liam attended the University of Notre Dame, where he eventually pursued a graduate program in psychology, and Thomas obtained a business degree from Florida State University.

Both Liam and Thomas returned to their beloved hometown. They re-connected at the aforementioned 10-year union, becoming best friends.

They often commiserate that society projects what it wants people to know, but real friends inwardly share what friends need to know.

Liam was a frequent guest at the Barrys' home in Coquina Key, a residential area nestled along the Bay in South St. Petersburg. It was almost as if Liam were family. He was affectionately called Uncle Liam, prior to his ordination, by Trey, his younger brothers, Brendan and Finn, and sister, Aiden.

Liam's star pointed north with a promising practice as a clinical psychologist in the Tampa Bay Area. He was a sole practitioner, specializing in mental health counseling and therapy. Liam became somewhat of a household name when he penned a series of articles entitled, "Helping your Children Cope with Bullying," in Psychology Today.

The articles gave him a platform and visibility to be the media darling when addressing incidents of school bullying. But it was not enough. His life felt incomplete. He was evolving spiritually, embracing grace and self-deprivation. It was not until he heard "the calling" to be a seminarian that he felt whole.

It made perfect sense for Fr. Liam to be at Trey's bedside. Trey was in and out of consciousness, slowly coming out of a comatose state. His eyes were re-focusing from myopia as morphine permeated his blood stream. However, even in his hallucinogenic state, he recognized the Roman collar and softly mumbled, «Thank God.»

Fr. Liam smiled effusively and placed his right hand on Trey's forehead to comfort him as if everything would somehow be ok. His serene countenance was reassuring for Trey at a moment when he needed assurance.

The priest's eyes then narrowed, manifesting a few strewn wrinkles on his forehead, as he spoke: "Young man, the good Lord has given you knew life. It is not yet your time. God has a plan for you on this Earth."

Trey emotionally needed the sweet ring of familiarity. Having his parents and Fr. Liam at arm's length afforded him a sense of solace in otherwise discombobulation that was his life. Fr. Liam flashed a light smile as he held Trey's right hand and pensively stared into his eyes.

But it was Liam's eyes that said so much more than mere words. In particular, his gaze, in combination with his facial expression, was empathetic and resolute as non-verbal communication. This was one of his greatest gifts, providing comfort, trust and a cathartic non-verbal communicative response from those whom he ministered.

Fr. Liam knew this was not the time to engage Trey. That intuitive sense comes from hearing hundreds of people bear their souls through confession and administering Last Rites for those dying. He was adroit at readily observing the signs associated with the aftermath of attempted suicide.

Trey appeared to be riddled with guilt, refusing to make eye contact with anyone at his bedside. Trey also was conflicted. On one hand, he seemed genuinely appreciative to be alive. But being alive meant an impending onslaught of questions in which his nightmarish life would be an open book.

Trey equivocated about Fr. Liam's presence too. He asked himself, "Was Fr. Liam here for an inquiry and some sort of judgment, or was his motivation to help me?"

Under normal circumstances, that question would be unfair to judge Fr. Liam's intentions.

But Trey could be forgiven for his distrust and cynicism. Fr. Liam was convinced he would have to earn Trey's trust with gentle assertiveness. That thought induced a slight smile as Fr. Liam recollected St. Francis DeSales' most famous quote: "There is nothing as strong as gentleness."

Fr. Liam intuitively knew when to assert himself and when to meld in the background. He stepped backward, gesturing to Thomas and Katharine to be at their son's bedside.

Thomas looked no younger than his actual age of 62. His thinning brown hair, peppered with gray, foretold male pattern baldness. He had sagging cheek bones and slumped shoulders.

Katharine was attractive for a nearly 60-year-old woman who had borne four children. Her physical appearance was mostly even with medium height and average weight. She assiduously took care of herself, working out at the local gym every week-day morning after attending Catholic mass. Her regimen included swimming several laps in an Olympic-size pool at the gym.

She distinguished her physical appearance with a bright rose appended to her medium-length brown-hair. The rose appeared as if it were cascading into a plume, mitigating her otherwise professional attire.

Katharine knew what she liked and stayed with it, rejecting the whims of women's fashion. The rose was a long-lasting staple of her appearance before she wore her first bra. Her mother, raised in an opulent southern family, convinced her daughter the appendage of a rose created a wholesome yet appropriate flair for ladies. The daughter dutifully complied, in part for her devotion to her mother.

As Katharine clutched her son's hand, she joyfully said, "Praise God," preening a bit with raw emotion in the essence of consanguinity. However, in the next moment, she reminded herself as any good Catholic to refrain from a high-pitched fervor of a charismatic believer.

Paraphrasing the famous quote from the father in the parable of the prodigal son, she softly said:

"Trey was dead and now he is alive."

For Thomas and Katharine, they had experienced the lowest of lows believing their son had committed suicide and the highest of highs that his life had been saved.

They were exhausted, sleeping barely a wink since Trey's attempted suicide. They also were guilt ridden, asking themselves why they did not heed signs Trey was on a destructive path.

They felt a heavy burden to be part of the solution for Trey's convalescence. This in part stemmed from the old adage they embraced: 'If you are not part of the solution, you are part of the problem."

But for them, it did not matter, at least in the immediate moment, how their son nearly died. What mattered is God had given him a second chance and a new beginning.

Chapter 4

A New Beginning

As Trey transitioned from myopia, his mind was attempting to process his new lived reality. "Oh my God," Trey murmured to himself. "How am I going to explain why I attempted to (commit suicide)?" He could not bring himself to complete the thought.

Trey was carrying Catholic guilt for his attempted suicide. And in this moment, he could not wrap his brain around his actions and take responsibility for what he had attempted. He wanted to disavow the attempted suicide, but intuitively knew he had to own it.

Trey feared no explanation would justify his actions for his parents, Fr. Liam and himself, yet he knew some sort of explanation would be in order for him to move forward in life.

The Barrys, devout Catholics, considered the taking of one's life as a gravely wrong moral action. In many respects, it had been the Holy Grail of the Church. They embraced the Catechism of the Church, which states in part, 'We are stewards, not owners, of the life God has entrusted to us. It is not ours to dispose of."

Trey was ashamed and remorseful as any good Catholic. Could he somehow save face with his parents, siblings, and close friends by putting his unthinkable act behind him and live life with a sense of normalcy? He wrung his hands as if he were beseeching forgiveness. He wondered if he could ever live again—really live as a well adjusted person of sound body, mind and spirit.

Trey knew the answer to the aforementioned question had to be a resounding yes. Anything less than that, he would have no chance of emerging from the sad and pathetic imbroglio that had become his life. And, if he had any realistic hope for quality of life, Trey presumed his convalescent journey would require him to confront personal demons.

Thomas and Katharine, in consultation with Fr. Liam, agreed Trey's initial therapy should include his siblings. Aiden, Brendan and Finn, nicknamed Finney, anxiously awaited interaction with their bed-laden brother.

Aiden's soft gaze met Trey's eyes. She then kissed his forehead and clutched his hand, while whispering, "You are in our thoughts and prayers. We love you."

Finn and Brendan talked with Trey as brothers do, telling him to recover so they can fish.

"King Mackerel will be running in a few weeks," Brendan said. "All we need is our big brother to drive the boat."

Trey managed a smile as Thomas and Katharine politely gestured for Aiden, Brendan and Finn to exit the hospital room.

As Trey's siblings were in the doorway, he managed to say, "Please don't be strangers. Visit me when you can."

They nodded in unison as Finn added, "You know we will, Trey!" Unequivocally, Trey knew his family would be his rock for him to rebuild his life. With that thought, he drifted into a sound sleep.

Katharine, who had slept on a couch in Trey's hospital room the previous evening. was exhausted as she studied Trey as he opened his eyes. She sensed Trey's guilt-ridden state of mind. She comforted him, holding his hand and rubbing his shoulders while expressing her love for him.

The sordid developments within the past 24 hours had hit Katharine and Thomas like a ton of bricks. As far as they had known, Trey was in Tallahassee serving as an intern under Rep. John Connolly. They did not know their son was suicidal, or at least that is what they were telling themselves. They were in disbelief when told Trey had driven from Tallahassee to St. Petersburg to end his life.

Now Katharine was attempting to address the reality of the situation. Leaning over her son, gently running her fingers through his long strands of hair, she whispered:

"For the love of God, why did you refuse to come see me and your father when you were troubled?" Trey's face was flush as he abruptly twitched, irritating nerves in the back of his neck and along his spinal column. It was a painful reminder of his fragility. Nevertheless, he took a deep breath as he shifted in his sedentary position. His body was suddenly a bundle of nerves as pent up emotions were released.

Finding his bearings, he responded: ""I tried to talk with you more than once. But mom, you did not want to hear it," Trey said. She sighed, attempting to conceal her irritation from the accusatory tone in his voice. Nevertheless, her son's comments burrowed in her heart.

As a devoted- loving mother, Katharine already blamed herself for not realizing Trey's vulnerability for attempted suicide. But she could see the sincerity in his eyes. He had made vague references about his challenges, but stopped short he was preparing to end his life.

The truth of the matter, Trey did not manifest typical signs of depression and injurious behavior associated with attempted suicide.

But Katharine, a self-professed queen of second guessing, was guilt ridden why her maternal intuitive senses did not spark premonition that something was awfully wrong with her son. As can often happen, Trey's careening path of desperation was without warning. However, in retrospect, there were latent warnings. He had become somewhat of a recluse. His occasional Kodak smile had all but disappeared.

Attempting to cope with the devastation of Trey's near-death experience, Katharine wanted to understand why her son attempted the unthinkable. Katharine told herself to listen and not be defensive.

Katharine attempted to avoid the possibility of exacerbating Trey's fragile psyche. Her outward appearance belied an internal pitter-patter of anxiety. Her heartbeat quickened, and she was unsettled in a moment of panic, not knowing how to respond to her son.

Katharine made a concerted effort to speak softly and slowly.

"Trey," she said, "I apologize from the bottom of my heart for not being there for you in your time of most need."

Trey held out his hands. Katharine clutched them with a death-like grip.

Newfound guilt and emotions, in combination with a mother's unconditional love for her son, was the impetus for the rush of energy within her. It was the kind of explosive chemical release enabling a mother to lift an end of a car to save her child pinned under a tire.

At this moment, Katharine did not realize her monolithic-type embrace was becoming painfully uncomfortable for Trey.

Initially reluctant to spoil the embrace, Trey finally said: "Mom, you are going to love me to death with that grip." He managed a grin and Katharine smiled, accentuating her facial lines.

Trey's comment reminded her of his double entendre when offering her a Mother's Day card and flowers a few years ago, "Nothing is too good for you, mom."

Katharine knew Trey's intent was the highest form of flattery a son could bestow on his mother as if no gesture or gift is befitting for her. But she was amused that his kind words could be interpreted that she is not worthy of any gift.

As Katharine unlocked her grip and composed herself, she realized the exchange of smiles might be a precursor for a new beginning. There was a silence before Trey peered at his mom in pensive thought.

"What have I done,?" Trey asked. There was an awkward silence. Katharine recoiled, not knowing how to respond to the question. She looked around the room seemingly in search of an answer. She recollected a recent news article in which a priest, presiding over the funeral of a teenager who committed suicide, suggested the deceased may not reach pass through the gates of heaven.

But Katharine also recalled Catholics can be forgiven for suicide under certain circumstances. She needed an expert in such matters as she stepped out of the hospital room and contacted Fr. Liam, who immediately picked up the call.

Fr. Liam wasted no time, making a bee line from St. Mary Catholic Church to the hospital. He entered Trey's room intending to exude a sense of hope and will to live.

"First and foremost," Fr. Liam said with serence countenance, "it is human to fail, but we should not be defined for our failures; No one wants to be judged solely based on his or her worst behavior.

"You are not a lost soul who can't receive reconciliation," Fr. Liam said. "You are here among us and can be resolved of your attempt to commit suicide."

Fr. Liam cathartically added: "You did not commit suicide. And, you now understand with your second chance to be among us on this Earth that suicide is permanency to a temporary problem, There likely were grave psychological disturbances that were beyond your control."

In Catholicism, Fr. Liam said, such disturbances can diminish the responsibility of the one who committed suicide or attempted suicide. Case studies suggest that the vast majority of suicides and attempted suicides stem from grave psychological disturbances, he said.

Fr. Liam's dark brown eyes narrowed for deliberate effect, then added, "Let's remember the correlation of attempted suicide and those who bullied you.

"Never forget you are not reprehensible for the tormenting actions of others," Fr. Liam said. "By others, I am referring to the perpetrators who refused to embrace Gospel Values that every person is of inestimable worth."

Fr. Liam continued, quoting Victor Hugo's Les Miserables: "If the soul is left in darkness, sins will be committed. The guilty one is not who commits the sin, but the one who causes the darkness."

Pausing, Fr. Liam stepped closer to Trey. "For the balance of your life, you can light a candle or curse the darkness," he said. " Always chase the light. So you see Trey, you are absolved of any sin because of the psychological disturbances inflicted on you by others who brought the darkness."

Fr. Liam insisted that in Trey's spiritual journey, determining a cause is essential for his emotional and mental state.

For the first time since Trey's attempted suicide, his facial expression did not portend his tormenting past. Fr. Liam then added with aplomb, "I give you my word, young man. We will get through this together."

Chapter 5

Trey's Recovery

Fr. Liam's clarion call was to be a spiritual advisor and confidant for Trey in his convalescent journey. No doubt, this would be a daunting-formidable challenge, necessitating his bailiwick of eclectic skills as a cleric, psychologist, counselor and friend.

The pastor's close relationship with the Barry family and his budding relationship with Trey demanded that.

Fr. Liam wanted his ministry to be driven to help people such as Trey. He abhorred the bureaucratic morass of a pastor's daily challenges with rudimentary operations of a parish, from building maintenance to personnel matters and everything in between.

But he realized Trey's new world would not be easy to navigate. He smiled when remembering the sage advice from a Jesuit professor: "If it were easy, anyone could do it and anything worth doing is challenging."

Fr. Liam was in search of solutions to combat the plethora of challenges in Trey's life. Among his priorities were to address Trey's recurring nightmares and haunting memories.

The following week, Fr. Liam entered Trey's hospital room. He was asleep, but restless, turning back and forth while murmuring incoherencies. As Fr. Liam listened intently, Trey's restlessness intensified into a riveting crescendo until he awakened and sat up in his bed. He was experiencing a panoply of feelings, from anger, empathy, to remorse.

Although the room was dark, Fr. Liam could see Trey wiping sweat from his brow with audible desperation in his voice as he asked no one in particular, "Go away. Leave me alone."

Fr. Liam assumed Trey was responding to the haunting memories of his perpetrators. After a paused silence, Trey asked the question again, this time with vociferous indignation in his voice. The pattern repeated itself again and again as Trey's voice pertinaciously intensified.

Fr. Liam told himself in pensive observance, "Ah, the sobering ring of familiarity."

He intuitively understood Trey's agitated state provided a window into his past.

"We have to identify the problem in order to provide a solution," Fr. Liam reminded himself. He believed Trey would need to move beyond the demons of his past in order to take the necessary steps to move forward in life.

Fr. Liam could no longer remain in esoteric silence. He flipped the light switch on and calmly called Trey by name as he approached him. He reached out to clutch Trey's hand, but Trey recoiled his arm brusquely.

Trey's veins vexed from his neck as he fervently shot back: "No one knows what it is like to be me!"

Fr. Liam knew this was not the time to engage in discourse with Trey. He simply wanted to subdue him.

But Trey was in a fervor pitch of protracted soliloquies, reminding himself that the horrors in his dreams were not fiction, but the lived reality of his misery.

"Those SOB's," Trey shouted to no one in particular. Fr. Liam decided to change tactics. Instead of attempting to quell Trey, he encouraged him to be cathartic in releasing pent-up demons.

In the next several minutes, Trey would have made old school sailors proud by screaming obscenities as if he were confronting his perpetrators of yesteryear. The emotional outbursts were so vociferous that orderlies arrived at Trey's room to tranquilize him.

Fr. Liam intervened. "That won't be necessary. Trey had an outburst. I assure you the worst is over and I will stay with him until he is calm."

The orderlies stayed with Trey to ensure he remained under control.

Fr. Liam had seen enough to know Trey would need to overcome daunting challenges to make a full recovery.

Fr. Liam sighed, knowing Trey's transition to eventually be of sound body, mind and spirit would likely be a protracted process of therapies counseling and other treatments.

His intuitive senses told him his approach would need to be utilitarian.

As Fr. Liam pondered his obligation to the Barry family and Trey in particular, he was reminded of the biblical principle: "When much is given, much is expected." He chuckled, which was a reflex reaction for him to cope with stress.

Fr. Liam then recollected an adage that always has provided solace for him when under duress: "The good Lord only gives us what we can handle."

Fr. Liam had all he could handle with Trey as a broken man with haunting memories and a combination of psychological impediments and sustained medical injuries.

Fr. Liam was connected to the medical community in the Tampa Bay Area and was determined to be at Trey's room when Paul Johnson, an orthopedic specialist. arrived.

Dr. Johnson, a thinly framed man with a salt and pepper permeated beard, was reputed for his off the cuff remarks. Fr. Liam wanted to interpret any comments that would be problematic for Trey to process.

Fr. Liam remained in Trey's room while Dr. Johnson was visiting patients. Eventually, Dr. Johnson arrived at Trey's room and cut to the chase:

"I have learned not to over promise and under deliver," he said, clearing his throat. "The last thing I want to do is give you false hope.

"But with that said, my prognosis suggests you should physically make a full recovery," he said. The muscular structure of the human body is resilient, but mental health is a completely different matter."

Fr. Liam looked downward, slumping his shoulders as if he were a model of reticence. This was his non-verbal gesture to not engage.

Fr. Liam did not want to encourage a discussion with Dr. Johnson at this time, particularly in Trey's presence. As Dr. Johnson exited, Fr. Liam comforted Trey:

"This is a process, There is no panacea or quick fix. Together with your family and support group, you will get through this."

In the immediate days ahead, a series of CAT scans were performed on Trey, as well as tending to a punctured lung, pinched nerves in his neck and cracked ribs. He was moved from the intensive care unit to general care and observation.

Two weeks later, Dr. Johnson informed Trey he would be released from St. Petersburg General Hospital, transitioning to outpatient therapeutic care.

Before Trey's release, he had unexpected visitors. Hearing a knock on the door, Trey looked at the doorway, and standing in it were Captain Garza and his crew, Zack and Jake.

Trey did not have many friends and he did not expect anyone other than his parents and Fr. Liam to visit him. Trey had ambivalent thoughts as his eyes focused on the trio.

"Were they friends or foes," Trey asked himself. He wanted to avoid any discussion with them about attempted suicide. They did not enter the room until invited to do so. Once in the room, they greeted Trey as Mr. Barry, gently offered their thoughts and prayers for his complete recovery.

They were altruistically motivated, but Trey was unprepared for Captain Garza's next move. He approached Trey and presented a card, which stated:

"Dear Trey -- We wish you fair winds and following seas. May your compass stay true and your anchor holds fast and strong as your bilges stay dry."

As Trey read the card, his eyes teared as he softly said he will not forget them and their sentiments. Trey was struck with the irony that Captain Garza, Jake, and Zack Jack were strong seafaring men, yet were humble and empathetic.

Other than his family, Trey was not accustomed to kindness. There were too many incidents to recount in which his name was never called for choosing sides for basketball, nor asked to join any friend group for that matter.

The extrication made him feel so lonely and vulnerable that he often slept in the fetal position as a teenager to ensure a sense of security.

Reflecting on the kindness from Captain Garza and his crew, Trey wondered whether a good deed can foster hope and faith in a world rife with evil.

As he gave this further thought, his mind and life experiences were telling him that a good deed does not necessarily wipe away a lifetime of abuse, but it can spawn hope. He so badly wanted to see the goodness in people. realizing a positive approach would bode well for his recovery.

Trey had learned a coping mechanism to pinch himself as a distraction from reliving the horrors of his past. And like women who forget about the pain associated with childbearing, Trey hoped his therapy would help him forget his wretched life fraught with unbearable humiliation and shame.

Chapter 6

Trey's Childhood Misery

Fr. Liam suggested the Barry family invite their friends and fellow parishioners from St. Mary's Catholic Church for a "Respect Life" celebration for Trey. The celebration was held at Maximo Park near O'Neill's Marina on St. Petersburg's Southside.

Conspicuously missing were Trey's former classmates. For all practical purposes, it was a joyous occasion. Recreational activities included paddle ball, corn hole, and volleyball. There was a bountiful spread of food and beverages.

Fr. Liam led a blessing emphasizing the sanctity of all human life without specifically mentioning Trey by name. Trey would have been uncomfortable with being the focal point of the benediction. The celebration served its purpose. People of faith gathered to rejoice and celebrate Trey's life.

Trey felt support. He was beginning to realize he was no longer alone.

But Thomas and Katharine were still in the dark about why their son catapulted from the Skyway. They wanted answers.

The Barrys had always been a close-knit family. Thomas and Katharine genuinely believed Trey was loved. There were so many nostalgic memories, from family vacations in the Florida Keys, to mundane picnics, watching sports, and supporting one another in various extracurricular activities.

One of their more amusing activities was for the children to compete with one another to determine who had the strongest stomach muscles. They laid on their backs, extending their legs inches off the ground while extending them. Aiden and Trey howled as they were no match for younger Brendan and Finn, both of whom casually fidgeted their fingers while holding their legs in place as if they did not have a worry in the world.

It was a silly game, but wholesome fun as Thomas and Katharine moderated the activity.

Thomas and Katharine had inculcated all for one and one for all mentality that the children embraced. They were there for one another.

Trey participated in high school football in which he ran to daylight as a running back with sprinter speed. He also participated in track, specializing in the 200-meters relay.

From the time Trey began wearing a male supporter, athletics afforded him a safe haven. Be it a football game or track, the rules were clearly defined within the field of competition and enforced.

Those who violated rules were penalized and repeat offenders were suspended, or even permanently banished from their sport. Rules and enforcement created a level playing field. For the duration of a football game or track meet, Trey was in a controlled environment in which the sport afforded him a proverbial bubble, extricated from the real world.

As is the case with virtually all siblings, there were occasional arguments, most of which stemmed from good natured ribbing and irritations that bubbled up in the heat of the moment.

They could step on one another's last nerve by playing music too loud, eating the last piece of chocolate, or borrowing a sibling's personal item without asking. It was all part of living in a large family.

But despite the typical brotherly and sisterly tensions, there was a loving-caring bond among them. They somehow knew the bonds would be sustained throughout their lives.

Trey's life was good when he was with his family. It was no coincidence when the Barrys returned from boating and camping vacations a few weeks before the beginning of each school year when Trey was a middle school student, his demeanor and persona morphed from a happy well-adjusted child to a neurotic mercurial and insecure youngster.

The thought of another school year with rogue classmates was enough for him to become isolated and withdrawn. He dreaded the thought of the incorrigible trio—Randy Carr, Juan Cantero, and Gillian Brock—making his life a living hell. Gillian especially was creepy. She was unmistakingly Gothic Her red eyebrows and spiked crimson hair were not merely a fashion statement. Her appearance projected a dark certitude in which she was reputed to hiss and caterwaul as if she were demonic.

They were perpetrated reprobates—young gangsters who pillaged and plundered, manifesting an insidious display of antipathy for victims who had never wronged them.

It was a badge of honor for the depraved sociopaths to target innocent victims. They were vile and dangerous, inflicting beatdowns as if they were an unlimited commodity.

There was no shortage of time and energy to extract abuse. This is what they did on any day, any time. Everything else was secondary.

In their inner circle, they dubbed themselves as despicable deplorables. They were recalcitrant and obstreperous, repugnant to their core and devoid of any compassion.

They always appeared to be on the prowl for the kind of low-hanging fruit that is easy prey. Trey fit that description to a tee.

They feasted on Trey's occasional malaprops and faux paws as fodder for him to be the brunt of endless practical jokes and punchlines.

In reality, Trey was no imbecile. He was an honor roll student with above-average intelligence, but he was mocked for his mental lapses and social awkwardness.

One such example was during recess playing dodgeball, Trey was quoted as saying he forgot to "dunk." Trey was not aware of former President

Ronald Regan's famous comment to First Lady Nancy – "Honey, I forgot to duck" after he was nearly fatally wounded by a gunshot.

Moreover, as Trey defended castigated classmates with a deep sense of conviction, he was a sacrificial lamb for Randy, Juan, and Gillian.

Trey deflected most of the insults from Randy, Juan, and Gillian as water off a duck's back.

But the marrow-deep excoriations kept coming.

This was especially so when they would rhythmically chant: "Trey sucks" as his eyes scanned for a vacant seat at lunch in the school's cafeteria.

Randy unabashedly attempted comedy at Trey's expense, asking if he needs directions on how to wear a jockstrap, or whether he can walk and chew gum at the same time. Regardless, Trey was a target as if he had a "punching bag" inscribed on his back.

But like drug addicts looking for their next fix, Randy, Juan, and Gillian took the ridicule and taunts to lower levels of depravity.

They had read on social media how students had bullied and taunted an Irish-born girl until she hanged herself in her parents' home in western Massachusetts. There were reports classmates continued to bully her after death, declaring she got what she deserved.

Her suicide whetted the insidious appetites of the St. Pete's gang of three to hatch a plan for Trey to be their trophy manifestation of death by induced suicide.

It was almost surreal as if Randy, Gillian, and Juan were bedeviled to move forward with Babylonian abandon, stoking fear and intimidation into the depths of Trey's psyche. Trey was like the proverbial ostrich burying his head in the sand. If he could not see them, perhaps the problem would be solved through osmosis.

In retrospect, Trey learned a painful lesson that ignoring a problem only makes it worse.

Trey could not have imagined what the trio had in store for him. But true to form, the spectacle was in the school cafeteria. As Trey entered the lunch room, Randy, Juan, and Gillian chanted a refrain that Trey was worthless and his life was not worth living.

They raised their hands with a thumbs up as a cue for their classmates to join in the public humiliation of Trey, who responded with a deer-in-the-headlights stare.

None of the classmates actively participated in Trey's torment.

But fear of not being the next victim reduced them to silence. They did not understand that one does not have to be an active participant in an evil act for it to prosper. They cravenly rolled over as their silent complicity empowered Randy, Juan, and Gillian to humiliate Trey.

By doing nothing, they were part of the problem, reprehensible as sycophants devoid of bravado independence. The threesome approached Trey, who was seated next to his classmates at a table in the school cafeteria.

Trey was on the precipitous end of peril as Randy directed him to stand atop the table to be displayed for the full effect of public shaming.

Trey, aghast, immediately recoiled, then intimidatingly did as he was told.

Trey stood awkwardly on the table. He felt so alone. As he began to choke back sobs, he saw his older sister. Aiden, exit the cafeteria with great celerity. Trey assumed she was attempting to track down the Dean of Students, Dr. Robert Butters.

Within minutes, Dr. Butters arrived at the cafeteria. He looked at the spectacle of Trey standing atop a table while Randy, Juan, and Gillian humiliated him. For a few moments, he thought Dr. Butters' presence would save him.

But Dr. Butters pivoted, exiting the cafeteria. At that moment, a dispassionate gaze fell on Trey. He was emotionally emasculated. Trey felt utterly defeated as he mentally and emotionally attempted to prepare for a verbal flagellation of the third degree.

It would be nothing less than a primordial highlight show featuring Trey's subjugation.

Randy's piercing green eyes narrowed as he flashed a mischievous smile before asking Trey, "Can we agree your sick and worthless life is not worth defending?" Trey hung his head in a depiction of effigy without nary a word.

"That's what I thought, Trey," Randy declared. "You have nothing to say because your existence in this world is meaningless."

Randy was laying the groundwork for his brazenly next move. With a devilish sneer that only Satan could fully appreciate, Randy casually asked Trey, "Can you do all of us a favor?" Trey was bamboozled by the question and hesitated. Before Trey answered, Randy added, "All of your classmates would like you to go home and blow your brains out. Can you do that for us, Trey?"

Randy was emotionally detached, sauntering over to Trey and casually asking him to kill himself with a bullet to his head as if he were asking for spare change or traffic directions.

But Randy had lit a match for incendiary implosion beyond his imagination. That question bewildered Trey to his core. It was as if an anvil had pierced his inner core. His hypothalamus, a small region of the brain located near the pituitary gland, sounded an alarm that his stress and anxiety were on overload.

Medical students are taught the hypothalamus instructs adrenal glands to release cortisol and adrenaline, both stress hormones.

Trey's eyes widened and eyebrows arched as his classmates silently fixated on him.

Not one of Trey's classmates objected to Randy's hideous question.

In Trey's mind, the silence of his classmates was their acquiescence for him to end his life. Trey's heart pulsated as if it would burst through his chest. In one moment he was his quintessential reticent self. The next moment he shot back, finding ferocity in no short supply.

Trey's face turned a tawdry color, twitching into a contorted frown. His eyes bulged with involuntary blinking as he was uncontrollably masking into someone he is not.

He suddenly was the anti-Trey as if he were morphing into a raw emotional state in which venomous hate spewed from every fiber in his body while raging adrenaline and endorphins intensified into a full froth of outward aggression.

That chemical implosion was the impetus for an impulsive uncontrollable outburst. Apocalyptically, Trey's moment had arrived. The veins in Trey's neck pulsated as he was on the verge of a blood-curdling macabre scream. His forehead and cheeks were crimson, manifesting the tempest boiling within him.

Trey pointed his fingers at Randy as if they were weapons. His voice, quivering, amplified into a high-pitched shrill with utter revulsion as if he were shouting for the heavens to hear:

"Go to hell you son of a bitch. You are a certifiable pathological demon who deserves to die."

And, then in one seamless motion, Trey leaped off the table and lunged at Randy, whose arms and neck were permeated with tattoos of skeletal remains.

But Trey was no match for Randy, who was reputed as a pugnacious thug.

As Randy was pummeling Trey into submission, Juan and Gillian jumped into the onslaught for overkill. Trey had a black eye, broken nose, and chipped tooth as sheriff deputies impeded the fracas.

Deputies had arrived on the school grounds at the behest of Dr. Butters.

But what no one could have predicted is Trey's unwillingness to turn the other cheek. For the first time in his life, he stood his ground and refused to relinquish his self-respect by tapping into a newfound fervor.

Despite the beat down and predation upon him, Trey was not submissive, at least not at this moment on this day. His courage to fight back unmasked an inner strength, a quality that mental health experts would use as an anecdote in his future recovery. Trey did not know it at the time, but this was his watershed moment, from lifelong submissive to formidable defender.

Trey was initially charged with assault, but that charge was dismissed. No charges were filed against Randy, Juan and Gillian. Incredulously, they received impunity, unless a one-week in-school suspension defined their punishment, which Trey also received.

And also inexplicably astonishing, bullying, public shaming, and exhorting Trey to kill himself warranted the same response as writing graffiti on a wall of a school building.

That decision was antithetical in the minds of Thomas and Katharine, who had taught their children to reap what they sow.

They had asked the Pinellas County School Board to override the school's leniency, arguing there ought to be a punishment beyond in-school suspension for particularly serious transgressions. But the school board backed the school's decision, defending policies in which discipline is limited to detention, in-school suspension, and out-of-school suspension for any non-criminal matter.

Adding insult to injury, the Pinellas County Sheriff's Office refused to regard the incident as a crime.

"Guess this is the cross we have to bear," said a jaded, dejected Thomas. He was soul-searching, trying to fathom how a cadre of thugs could receive impunity for unconscionably bullying his son.

"It was a manifestation of malevolence," Thomas said to no one in particular.

Katharine knew her husband was anguishing, embracing him and whispering, "We have to concentrate on our son and not be caught up in punishment."

Thomas slowly nodded his head.

Fr. Liam would later affirm Trey for attempting to defend himself against the onslaught.

"For you, Trey, and all of us, there is no progress without struggle. You must discern what you want, then fight for it,' Fr. Liam said in a stentorian voice.

But Trey pushed back: "I just want people to leave me alone. Is that too much to ask for?"

Fr. Liam didn't want to engage in debate, simply saying: "I hear you, Trey. You have a right to live your life, but hopefully, through the grace of God you have the right to defend yourself as of inestimable worth in the human race."

But the priest went one step further: "Pray for Randy, Juan, and Gillian. There is a deep void in their lives. Pray the power of the Holy Spirit will fill that void with compassion as fellow brothers and sisters in Christ."

Fr. Liam explained: "Each of us must "lose" at something and then we begin to develop the art of losing in which we acquire the grace from God to compassionately respond to the trials and tribulations in life.

"Most of us can be a good version of ourselves in good times; the challenge is to respond with God's grace when there is adversity," Fr. Liam said.

The cleric continued; "You were victimized, preyed upon and bullied unmercifully. But let's not assume the incident has been easy for the perpetrators. No one wants to be defined based on his or her worst behavior. It could very well be that Randy, Juan, and Gillian were at their very worst when they shamelessly bullied you."

There was little doubt Trey's humiliation left psychological scars that would haunt him, in one degree or another, for the rest of his life. Those scars explained why Trey instantly flinched at the mere mention of Randy's name.

But Fr. Liam believed there was a spiritual remedy for Trey to be at peace within his life.

"It is in silence with the Lord that He speaks to us," Fr. Liam said.

Trey nodded in approval, recollecting a profound sense of serenity and calmness upon him while praying to the Lord during adoration.

Trey heeded Fr. Liam's suggestion to avoid social media and the negative opinions and political comments associated with it. An enhanced prayer life, coupled with avoiding social media, was the blueprint for a healthier life.

Trey eventually no longer awakened in the middle of the night in a cold sweat, confronting demons of his past.

The psychologist in Fr. Liam told him that a single cataclysmic event would not lead to attempted suicide.

But if Trey were to continue to be victimized by the likes of Randy, Juan, and Gillian, then he inevitably would be a tortured-broken soul – a metaphorical Humpy Dumpy.

"This would explain the attempted suicide," Fr. Liam told himself, acknowledging there comes a breaking point in which there is no will for recovery.

Fr. Liam knew he had to glean whether there were other tormenting episodes.

But even if there were other episodes, Fr. Liam would cling to a ray of hope:

Throughout most of Trey's life until the days leading up to his attempted suicide, he had demonstrated an abiding will and resolve to live life on his terms.

Chapter 7

Bad to Worse

Nearly six years after the horrific debacle of Randy, Juan, and Gillian, Trey no longer was looking over his shoulder for the next bully. He had been free of devastation and learned to accept rudeness and alienation as a way of life. He was beginning to come out of his shell, having asked a girl, Felicia, to high school prom. The experience was bittersweet.

Felicia was 18 going on 28. She insisted Trey obtain a fake ID so they could imbibe cocktails before arriving at the prom. With Felicia's help, Trey acquired the bogus ID.

Truth be known, she only agreed to be his date because she wanted to find out whether his choir boy persona was an act. She soon found out. While at a Gulf Front Restaurant on St. Pete Beach, a server asked Trey if he wanted a cocktail. Trey answered "yes," specifically asking for a shrimp cocktail.

At that moment, Felicia lost all interest in Trey. In her view, he was beyond a stiff shirt. He was a complete geek and nerd. They proceeded to the prom, only for obligatory reasons. She insisted Trey have her home before midnight.

Trey later found out Felicia was seen partying with friends in the early morning hours. But even a lousy date was no reason for despair.

He was an inconspicuous high school student, blending into the crowd, not calling attention to himself. He was ok with anonymity.

Randy, Juan, and Gillian, however, were indelibly within the deep recesses of his mind. Rand especially was in Trey's head, imagining Randy at a street corner or grocery store.

In Trey's mind, Randy was ubiquitous.

But eventually, Trey realized time heals all wounds as Randy became a distant memory. Years had passed since he had been bullied.

It was only when he was reminded of middle school that ugly memories haunted him. And even then, he trained himself to associate his mind with any nostalgia to re-channel his thoughts.

As a recent high school graduate who enrolled at the University of Tallahassee-Pensacola, Trey was attempting to immerse into college life.

But he had no social network. Thomas and Katharine encouraged him to pledge a fraternity. Trey naively presumed he would acquire an instant social life with newfound frat brothers. He was convinced pledging was win-win.

Trey was unaware rogue fraternities were reputed for hazing pledges. Unfortunately, he was hoodwinked into pledging a fraternity of misfits and wannabes. They were the dregs of Greek Life because none of the brothers had the allure to be considered by more upscale fraternities.

No one referred to them by their official Greek title. On campus, particularly in Greek Life, they were called "Mud Dogs," a dubious moniker coined in the backwoods of Louisiana for swamp people.

The stigma stuck because the fraternity did nothing to distinguish itself otherwise. They were hell-bent on any recognition, good, bad, or indifferent. They mostly reveled in debauchery, from excessive drinking, underage drinking, audacious stunts, and repulsive dares.

Their parties were crazy wild and coeds knew it. That is why very few females were in attendance. However, the few remaining little sisters of a sorority on the brink of closure were frequent guests. It was a match made in hell. Decorum was eschewed for boundless depravity.

It was little surprise that all 13 of the brothers suffered from relative degrees of little man syndrome. They were glaring examples of so badly wanting to be big men on campus. This proved to be a toxic combination in which they felt superiority by beating down and humiliating pledges.

Unbeknownst to Trey, a brother of the fraternity, Hiram, and a little sister of the sorority, Shelly, conspired to put the new pledges through a twisted-criminal-induced week of hell.

Shelly contrived for one of her sorority pledges, Mallory, to lure Trey to the Tallahassee Sinks, which were caverns with deep ravines, for a late-night swimming party.

Mallory and Trey knew one another from a political science course. They occasionally passed each other coming and going from Sally Hall, a co-ed dorm. Men were on even-number floors; girls on odd-number floors.

Mallory often sashayed when she walked, accentuating her sinewy-petite figure. Her glossy jet-black hair complemented her slender-unblemished face. She had a smile that could light up a room.

It was no wonder Trey and other male students were smitten with her. Trey's shyness and insecurities inhibited him from flirtatious conversation or even conversing with her beyond greetings and salutations.

But he was a romantic at heart, One of his favorite pastimes was to listen to a genre of love songs from the 1970s. His favorites were Love will Keep us Together from the Captain and Tennille and the theme song from the movie, Love Story.

Gullible to a fault, Trey was swooned off his feet by attractive women who exhibited the slightest interest in him. When such a woman parlayed her seductiveness into charm, he was putty in her hands.

Suffice it to say, when Mallory beckoned, Trey did not hesitate to accept her invitation to accompany her and a group of college students for a late-night swim.

Trey did not know Mallory was the bait for him to be the center attraction in Hiram and Shelly's tangled web of deceit. As Mallory and

Trey arrived at the caverns in her Mini Cooper, there were six other men and five women near the water.

Trey and Mallory watched the others divest their clothes and frolic in the water. Trey was not prepared for skinny dipping. He was not a free spirit and was uncomfortable with public nudity.

But he acquiesced at Mallory's behest.

"Don't be such a stick in the mud,» Mallory said with a conspiratorial giggle as she wistfully teased while stripping down to her birthday suit.

Trey was aghast at Mallory's lack of inhibitions to be nude with people she met mere weeks ago when pledging.

But he would go along to get along, feigning he was ok with what he considered Mallory's wild side. Trey was having second thoughts about whether Mallory was the wholesome girl next door he had envisioned.

Mallory then approached him, running her fingers through his thick tousled hair while unbuttoning his shirt. Once shirtless, he hesitantly slipped out of his shorts.

"Shall we?" Mallory asked with a mischievous smile as she grabbed his hand and they ran into the water. Minutes later, Mallory distracted Trey as the others returned to the beach and dressed.

When Mallory heard Shelly prescriptively blow a whistle, she turned to Trey, giving him a penitent look before saying, "Please don't be too upset with me."

She then briskly exited the water and donned her bikini.

Trey followed Mallory to the beach and scanned the muddy shoreline for his clothes. His heartbeat quickened as his shorts and T-shirt were nowhere in sight. He then observed flames emanating from a nearby fire pit.

Trey was in full panic mode as he witnessed Shelly holding his clothes over a fire. In an instant, she dropped the garments on the scorching flames. The thinly veiled cloth of his t-shirt and swimming trunks were charred to ashes within minutes.

Trey swallowed hard, followed by a sick feeling. He was in an acute state of nauseousness, realizing his victimization was from a conspiratorial betrayal in which Mallory's seductive kit was the allure for him to be in this God-forsaken predicament.

Trey realized his public shaming was just beginning. If there were a crack in the shoreline for which he could disappear below the surface, he would certainly have done so.

But in reality, Trey was on full display. His clothed peers circled him to gawk, ridicule, and embarrass him. Mortified, his face was flush, appearing as if he were anemic. His eyes were sullen. He looked downward to avoid eye contact with everyone.

Trey begged for a towel, but the cadre of reprobates had no intention to give his request any consideration.

Shelly was the ringleader in antics gone wrong. Her debaucheries were beyond brazen. She sarcastically uttered remarks about Trey's genitalia and overall nude state. The staging of his fragility and vulnerability allowed her to revel with lecherous delight and delve into her innermost hedonistic urges.

She was inebriated with a toxic cocktail of authority and power, satisfying her prurient appetite to publicly shame and humiliate.

Shelly gaped at Trey, her face inches from him, then she asked with an audible snort, "Do you have anything to say before we begin?"

"Begin what?" Trey asked, pleading for a modicum of modesty.

"Don't worry poor boy, you will be dressed in no time," Shelly said, cackling at her false promise.

In actuality, Trey's nudity was not his only problem. As others held Trey down, Shelly cut his hair and shaved his head but for a half-inch swath along the middle of his scalp. There he stood au natural with his hair reduced to a poor imitation of a mohawk.

The others, except Mallory, embraced Trey's public shaming as if it were a cult-like ritual. Mallory had been told she would become a little sister if she convinced Trey to skinny dip. It was her understanding there would be a few awkward moments for Trey as he remained in his birthday suit while the others were dressed.

Mallory knew she had been duped and responded with a sharp rebuke and agitation in her voice as she stood face-to-face with Shelly:

"This was not part of the plan. I did not sign up for this. Shaving Trey's head is crossing the line. It probably constitutes some kind of crime."

Mallory did not know at this moment she had lit the match for Shelly to implode with incendiary tumultuousness, giving new meaning of hath hell for the fury of a woman scorned.

"Know your place, bitch," Shelly shot back. "You are nothing more than a pledge and we can do far worse to you than what we did to your little boyfriend."

Mallory's heart pulsated as if it would implode, but she refused to back down.

"How about I call the police?" Mallory threatened as her voice ascended with raw indignation. This further incensed Shelly, whose blue eyes glared and nostrils flared as she commanded the others to respond with deafening vociferousness.

Mallory was mortified as the others played their part with thunderous condemnation of her.

"Chant Mallory's name if she should be publicly humiliated," Shelly said as if she were conducting a symphony of caustic-rhythmic condemnation of Mallory.

In a unified cadence, others blindly followed Shelly's dictum as if they were unadulterated sycophants.

Chants were enunciated phonologically – MAL—LOR-EE - that had an eerie-creepy pronouncement as if she were one of the women to be burned at the stake in the aftermath of the Salem Witch Trials.

Shelly and her followers were in a frenzy for their brand of justice. She did not have to remind them that to do anything less would be an unforgivable transgression.

The pledges, fraternity brothers, and sorority sisters had to look no further than Trey and Mallory to be reminded they did not want a similar fate.

The sheer volume and fervor of the chants sealed Mallory's fate.

Shelly knew she could take depravity to a new low and none of her subordinates would break rank.

There was not an iota of mercy in Shelly's heart for Mallory's defense of Trey. With that, Shelly directed the others to surround Mallory as she was divested of her shorts and T-shirt in one seamless motion.

As Mallory's eyes began to tear up, Shelly said, "Don't cry poor little Mallory. We are not through with you yet."

Shelly gestured for two fraternity brothers to hold Mallory as her hair too was shaved into a mohawk, but with a twist. Shelly, having a dark soul that would delight Satan, smiled with devilish delight as she rubbed a mixture of hair gels, paste, and sprays onto Mallory's scalp. She meticulously left long strands within the swath of her mohawk so they would monolithically stand upright.

In an attempt to break Mallory, Shelly held a compact mirror in front of Mallory's face. Predictably, she began to sob as she could barely recognize herself. She looked like an absolute freak that only a punk rocker could admire.

Mallory begged Shelly to shave the hideous Mohawk. She was pleading for her head to be completely shaved.

But Shelly wanted Mallory to feel as much shame and humiliation as possible. Shelly was not yet done.

As Mallory's head was held by two sets of hands as if it were in a vice grip, Shelly slithered a razor across Mallory's eyebrows until they were no more.

In the aftermath, she felt so hideous and pathetic. Her sans eyebrows and mohawk made her look more like a space alien than an attractive young woman.

This was precisely Shelly's objective – to transform Mallory from a modern-day Sandra Dee to a Gothic-looking freak.

Shelly reveled in the remaking of Mallory, destroying her appearance as a put-together young lady.

For Shelly, this was a predilection. She had neither the etiquette nor the beauty to compete with Mallory and other women like her.

In Shelly's warped mind, she had won a competition in which she had all of the leverage over a once attractive college coed who had been debased in a hideous sideshow.

What Shelly did not know is Mallory blossomed after her 18th birthday as a senior in high school. Until that time, she could have related to a verse in Janis Ian's Seventeen: "To those of us who knew the pain of valentines that never came and those whose names were never called when choosing sides for basketball."

As an adolescent, she was an introvert, insecure about the acne permeating her face, crooked teeth, and an overbite that orthodontics would correct. When her facial complexion exfoliated, complementing her glistening white-perfectly straight teeth, her self-confidence soared.

For Shelly, there was no such blossoming, but she craved attention, any kind, which led to her bad girl reputation.

Shelly had an entourage of wannabe bad girls, but none of them could hold a candle to her depths of depravity

Trey and Mallory were led to a human gauntlet in which a row of fraternity brothers was flanked by a line of sorority sisters. Their positioning was reminiscent of the famous scene in the Hungarian film, "Round-Up," in which a woman was flogged while running through a gauntlet sans clothing.

But there would be no running through the gauntlet for Trey and Mallory. As Shelly amplified, "Ladies before gentlemen," Mallory was positioned at the front of the gauntlet. "Let the fun begin," Shelly said as Mallory began her walk of shame.

Within moments, fraternity brothers grabbed her limbs, momentarily holding her in place while sorority sisters pummeled her buttocks. This was repeated as she made her way through the elongated gauntlet.

At that point, she fell to her knees, sobbing from the humiliation and the pain inflicted on her.

But Trey refused to give Shelly and her degenerate cohorts any savage delight as he stoically endured the gauntlet.

For Trey and Mallory, the nightmare was only beginning. They were forced to stand next to Hiram's flatbed truck. A rope was tied from the rear bumper of the truck to their wrists.

As Hiram and Shelly jumped into the cab of the truck, she shouted, "You reap what you sow."

While Trey and Mallory walked behind the truck, he leaned closer to Mallory and whispered, "I will never forget what you did for me this evening. I know we are not to judge, but I've got to believe Shelly will burn in hell one day."

Mallory slowly nodded her head. She believed if there was any justice, Shelly would pay for her diabolical ways.

Mallory then audibly responded to Trey, " I did not do this for you. I would have done this for anyone."

Trey cocked his head slightly to the side as he looked nowhere in particular, then added: "Just the same, thank you."

Mallory could only bring herself to say, "You can do me a favor, please do not look at me."

As the truck slowly moved down a secondary road in dire need of repair, Trey sensed Mallory was emotionally broken to her core.

For Mallory, it was not merely the forced nudity. That was bad enough. But having her natural beauty eviscerated as if she were a wretched villain in a comic strip was more public shaming and indignity than she could bear.

At this moment, Trey wanted to do something – anything – to help Mallory. One of his favorite quotes from Martin Luther King was ringing in his ears: "Anytime is a good time to do something right."

As if he had an epiphany, Trey yelled for the truck to stop. Hiram stopped the vehicle and sharply pulled the handbrake in frustration. Shelly turned to him and said, "This better be good."

She exited the truck and barked at Trey, "Are you some kind of masochist? What do you want us to do to you now?"

Trey was slow to respond, then said, " I don't know if you have thought this through. If we are arrested for public nudity, we will be forced to implicate you, Hiram, and the others."

Shelly with hands on hips, asked, "So, what is your point?" "I am simply asking," Trey said, "for us to be clothed so we are not arrested for public indecency."

Shelly snickered before saying, "I think we can handle this." She signaled for Hiram to fetch an old T-shirt in the cab of the truck. Hiram, anticipating Shelly's thoughts, ripped the shirt into thinly veiled strips.

In short order, ropes were around the waists of Trey and Mallory. Shelly then tied strips of cloth to the ropes, covering their loins and intergluteal clefts.

To the casual observer, Trey and Mallory no longer were completely nude. But for the discerning eye, the strips of cloth did not serve their intended purpose.

Even so, Mallory's eyes met Trey's line of vision. She could see the sincerity in his eyes. She gazed at him as if to say scantily clothed is better than no clothing. She intuitively knew Trey had initiated the request for her.

Mallory realized she had emanated a vibe of utter fragility and a deep-seated moroseness, which Trey sensed with great empathy.

As Hiram and Shelly jumped inside the truck, they cackled as they referred to Trey and Mallory as Tarzan and Topless Jane. Eventually, the truck slowly rolled into a gas station at the corner of 319 and Capital Circle.

Trey and Mallory were untied from the truck and instructed to make a run for it, which they did. They still had 5.5 miles to transverse before arriving at Sally Hall. As they approached the store, there was no one on the premises, except for the store clerk.

Mallory quipped to Trey, "Maybe I should wait outside while you talk to the clerk."

Mallory did not want to endure the indignity of the clerk casting judgment on her.

But Trey answered, "There is no way I am going to leave you alone in this God-forsaken place. A couple of thugs passing by could spot you and get the wrong idea."

Mallory reluctantly accompanied Trey into the store. He approached the counter as the clerk, Mario Arza, a middle-aged Hispanic man, was busying himself. Mr. Arza looked up when he heard Trey announce, "Excuse me, sir, excuse me, sir."

Mr. Arza appeared startled as he saw Trey and Mallory standing before him in practically all their glory but for the thinly veiled loin cloth.

Their nudity and mohawks, particularly Mallory's spiked hair standing atop her scalp, made them a sight for sore eyes.

"You have got to be kidding me," the clerk said. The look in his eyes was of disgust. "Is this some kind of sick joke?" Trey attempted to clarify, "This is no joke. I can assure you of that."

As Trey attempted to tell his story, Mr. Arza interrupted him in mid-sentence:

"I don't have time for this," he said. "Get your naked asses out of my store."

Mr. Arza glared at Mallory, adding, "You could be a cute girl." His voice trailed off. "But you must be a real slut to parade in my store buck naked. If you were my daughter, I would take a leather strap to your backside."

His dark brown eyes squinted as he leaned toward Mallory, then said emphatically, "You would not be able to sit down for a week." Now get out of here."

As Trey and Mallory exited the store, a couple of rednecks pulled into the parking lot in an older-model pickup truck. They had nothing better to do than joy ride to the convenience store on a Friday evening. One of the young men exiting the truck spat tobacco on the pavement, then looked up, saw Trey and Mallory, and uttered: "Look, what we have at 3 o'clock."

Both men quickly approached Trey and Mallory. One of the men, Billy Bob, pinched Mallory on her buttocks. She swatted his hand away. Billy Bob stared into her blue eyes, then said, "It is not as if you are properly dressed or anything. Hell, you are walking around like some kind of slut."

For Mallory, the insults kept coming. She was on the verge of a breakdown. But to get through this ordeal, she had to exude an outward bravado.

Trey took her hand and they began to walk toward the highway. Billy Bob jumped in the truck and urged the other man, Geoffrey, to do the same.

"Watch and learn," Billy Bob said with a wink. He pulled the truck ahead, just a few feet behind Trey and Mallory. He then depressed the truck's high beams.

Billy Bob turned to Geoffrey as if he were thoroughly satisfied with himself, then opined, "This is our movie for tonight. It is called "Freak Show."

As Trey and Mallory walked, she turned to him and said, "This is impossible. I can't do this, having two Neanderthals gawk at my naked backside."

Her comment moved Trey to approach the truck, confronting Billy Bob and Geoffrey: "What in the hell is your problem?" Trey said. "Only a couple of perverts would do something like this."

Trey's comments elicited the ire of Billy Bob and Geoffrey. Billy Bob put the truck in park, opened the door, and punched Trey, knocking him down. Geoffrey made a beeline to Mallory, grabbing her by the arms and forcing her into the truck.

This prompted Mr. Arza, watching the public torment of Trey and Mallory, to shout, "Let her go or I will call the police!"

Trey was groggy but was heartened to hear the word police. In truth, the clerk had no intention of calling the police. He had stolen goods on the premises and did not want the police sniffing around.

But the bluff spooked Billy Bob and Geoffrey, both of whom were small-time criminals with rap sheets. As Trey and Mallory continued their hellish journey to Tallahassee, they walked on the pavement when no vehicles were in sight.

They eventually spotted a small farmhouse in the distance.

"Let's see if there is a barn," Trey said. "Hopefully we can rest a while and not be detected." Trey's words were a premonition. As they were approaching an old barn, animals heard them. A dog barked and a horse whinnied. While attempting to open the barn door, Trey and Mallory saw a small light in the distance.

Within moments, they could see the silhouette of a man holding a lantern. Trey and Mallory were in the sight of an elderly man dressed in suspenders holding a shotgun. The man pointed the gun at Trey and Mallory, who were standing together, then pointed to a nearby sign. The man pulled a flashlight from his pocket and shone it on the sign, which stated: "Trespassers will be shot on sight."

Trey immediately broke his silence with his best effort to be a backwoods Southerner.

"Sir, we don't mean any harm. We've been stripped nude from a bunch of hoodlums and forced to somehow make our way back home." The man walked a few feet closer to them. Trey stood in front of Mallory.

"I don't know what to make of this," the man said before spitting tobacco near his feet. "Your story does not explain much."

"What do you mean sir?" Trey asked. The man lowered the gun to his side, rubbed his head, then added: "I may be getting senile, but your girlfriend is not only nude, but she looks like some kind of a freak."

The man then raised his gun and ordered Mallory to approach him. She was petrified but did what the man asked.

The man asked Mallory, "May I touch your head?" Mallory could not bring herself to audibly reply but simply nodded. He then rubbed his fingers along her spiked mohawk and looked downward as if he were in a pensive state, then uttered: "For a young woman to parade on my property like this, she must be on some wild ride."

Mallory knew explaining the lived reality was an exercise in futility. "I tell you what I am going to do," the man said, spitting another wad of tobacco. "I will give you 30 seconds to get off my land. And, you best not come back."

Trey and Mallory were exhausted. But fear is a great motivator and they ran like deer to exit the farmer's property. Within moments they were walking on Highway 319. Seeing headlights from a distance, they scampered to the brush along the roadway, inconspicuously lying on the ground.

The humiliation and judgment from strangers were more than they could bear, especially for Mallory. But there was a price to pay for preserving what little self-respect they had left.

The soles of their feet, already tender and oozing blood from miles of walking, were rife with sandburs and thorns from the brush. After vehicles passed, they would return to the shoulder of the roadway and attempt to pluck the sandburs from their feet.

Trey was not sure he and Mallory would be able to continue walking. He told her when the next car approached, he would flag it down. Thirty minutes or so later, a dark-colored sedan approached. Trey ventured to the center of the two-lane roadway and waived his hands frantically.

The sedan pulled over to the side of the road. A tall-slender man exited the vehicle and drew a gun, directing Trey to put his hands behind his head and kneel. Thought of an execution-style killing flashed through his mind.

Mallory, standing on the shoulder of the road, screamed. The man with a gun pointed a spotlight at Mallory, ordering her to show her hands. Mallory was ordered to approach the man, which she did.

As Mallory was within a few feet of the man, she audibly gasped that he had a gun. She feared a gun-toting predator would rape her.

Her frightened state of mind prevented her from seeing past the gun. She did not realize at that moment the man was clad in a uniform and was a sheriff's deputy.

Deputy Colin Brennan flashed his handheld Q Beam at Trey and Mallory. He could see embarrassment and humiliation on their faces. He then placed them in the back seat of his patrol car.

As the deputy drove to a 24/7 Walmart, he told Trey and Mallory that dispatch had received a call from one of the locals reporting two trespassers.

"Based on the description of a young man and woman in the buff, I had a pretty good hunch a young man and woman would be on the shoulders of Highway 319," Deputy Brennan said.

Trey and Mallory looked at each other, slowly nodding their heads.

"Thank God the old man made the call," Mallory said.

As Deputy Brennan parked the police cruiser at Walmart, he asked Trey and Mallory to lie low. They did so silently. Moments later Mallory broke the silence by gesturing the sign of the cross in the Holy Trinity – the Father, Son, and Holy Spirit -- thanking God they are alive and well.

Trey echoed Mallory's words, adding, "Thank you, Lord, for watching over us. Students die on college campuses each year from hazing incidents." Clutching one another's hands, they pensively gazed into each other's eyes. It was a moment neither Trey nor Mallory would forget.

Within minutes, the deputy returned with two cotton shorts, T-shirts, and a pair of sandals for each of them. Trey and Mallory quickly dressed themselves. Then Deputy Brennan launched into a narrative intended to elicit Trey's and Mallory's cooperation in a police investigation.

"Each of you understands public nudity is a crime," the deputy said. Trey and Mallory nodded emphatically. We will have no choice but to charge both of you with public indecency unless there is evidence of forced nudity."

Trey and Mallory were aghast. "Are you kidding me?" Mallory said incredulously, Deputy Brennan responded, "This is the harsh reality.

Both of you need to direct us to those responsible for this act or suffer the consequences."

Trey and Mallory could lawyer up in which mum's the word with law enforcement, or implicate Hiram, Shelly, and their accomplices.

Trey and Mallory knew Hiram, Shelly and their posse of misfits were more than capable of extreme vindictiveness. They looked at one another as if they had no real choice but to exonerate themselves by implicating their perpetrators.

Then Trey spoke. "Deputy Brennan, we will cooperate.'"

Deputy Brennan looked at Mallory, who was less than enthusiastic. She glared at the deputy, then added, "I will do whatever I have to."

"We will need each of you to provide a detailed statement as to the incident," Deputy Brennan told them. "A detective will be in contact."

Deputy Brennan drove Trey and Mallory to their residence, Sally Hall, which is located on the University of Pensacola-Tallahassee campus. He offered to accompany them to their separate rooms.

But Trey and Mallory begged off, not wanting extra attention or walking with a uniformed deputy. As they exited the police cruiser, Deputy Brennan gave each of them caps.

"Take these to cover the top of your scalps," Deputy Brennan said. Hopefully, no one will notice your shaved necklines."

Trey and Mallory nodded to the Deputy in appreciation and then made their way to the ground-level elevator while not detected by another human.

It was bad enough they had to endure public humiliation and shaming, but they did not want to have to relive that hell by having dorm residents mock them for their hideous mohawks. Fortunately, in the wee hours of Sunday morning, only Trey and Mallory were in the lobby.

Trey rode the elevator to the fifth floor, where Mallory departed to her room. He then took the elevator to the second floor, walking through the corridor to room 217.

In moments, he was in his room, secure, safe, and undetected. He heard his phone beep. A text from Mallory confirming she too arrived at her room undetected.

The next day Detective Bob Lowry directed Deputy Brennan to schedule an interview for Trey and Mallory to recount the incident.

Lowry was a cop's cop. He was known as the Leon County Sheriff's version of Danny Reagan of the acclaimed Blue Bloods television series. But he was neither politically astute nor capable of a cooperative spirit to build relationships within and outside the Sheriff's Office.

His approach was "my way or the highway." He did not care much whether he was well-liked. What he did care about was making arrests and having suspects turn on one another. He rationalized his actions even if they were the enemy of the good.

True to form, Detective Lowry was like a dog with a bone to coerce Mallory into signing a statement to incriminate Shelly and Hiram. He sensed Mallory was so traumatized over the public humiliation that she simply wanted to take the path of least resistance. Furthermore, the detective was betting on her to be intimidated into signing a statement of cooperation.

But Detective Lowry's modus operandi did not meld with State Attorney Butch Davis, who was reputed as a tough prosecutor with a folksy style and charm of a Southern politician.

That combination had served him well for decades. He knew where the political mines were and did his due diligence to circumvent implosion. One such example was his symbiotic relationship with the University of Pensacola-Tallahassee in which he needed the university more than it needed him.

Davis, a Tallahassee native whose family was steeped in southern politics, fully understood alienating the university and its fan base would end his political career in the capital city. This explained why he avoided prosecuting university athletes unless they committed felonies in broad daylight in the presence of eyewitnesses.

But the Leon County Sheriff's Office stoked the flames of condemnation against Greek Life. No longer were fraternities protected under the veil of secrecy. Enraged parents whose children died or were brutally hazed by rogue fraternities were pushing back by forcing universities and legislatures to publicize infractions, rein in egregious behavior, and strengthen criminal penalties after injuries and deaths.

Although rogue fraternity behavior had resulted in few criminal or civil consequences, the political winds were changing. No longer were allegations merely from a victim. Cell phones and video cameras were capturing incriminating evidence.

Trey and Mallory were caught in a power struggle with the Sheriff's Office, the State Attorney's Office, and the U.S. Department of Justice.

The U.S. Department of Justice had been investigating the University of Pensacola-Tallahassee and a plethora of universities across the nation for tolerating sexual discrimination and violence on college campuses.

Byron Cooley, a DOJ prosecutor who was charged with leading the investigation, was on a mission. He viewed rogue fraternities and street gangs as the same. Each embraced loyalty, brotherhood, and initiation.

Cooley, a thinly framed, diminutive man looked as if he could have been on the cover of GQ magazine. He had blue-eyed and blond hair, which always was slicked back as if he just showered. He wore two-piece Gucci suits with a silk tie that usually was skewed along a cut-a-long collar.

On an assistant attorney general's salary, Cooley actually could afford Gucci suits. He did not have a family to support and embraced Alex Agassi's mantra – image is everything.

Aside from occasional drooping posture, Cooley had aged well and looked the part of a frat boy as he approached his 35th birthday.

Cooley was on a crusade to make nefarious fraternities pay for their transgressions. In Cooley's mind, he gave no quarter to fraternities and rejected all forms of hazing, even those beginning innocently enough.

Cooley believed fatalities often began with mundane hazing, forcing pledges to do laundry and other domestic chores that escalated to a point of no return.

Inevitably there should come a point," Cooley said, "in which universities should shut down Greek Life and not let them open unless they can prove health and safety are paramount. And, if there is a hazing incident after that, they are suspended indefinitely."

There was no shortage of cases. Cooley's office had received voluminous reports detailing how pledges stripped to their briefs were forced outside in the dead of winter, nearly dying from hypothermia. And in other cases, pledges either were forced to ingest so much beer and liquor that they died from alcohol poisoning, or forced to inhale canisters of Nitrous Oxide, or a "whippet," leading to death by asphyxiation.

Regardless of the variances in the incidents, they had a commonality: exploiting vulnerable college students for hedonistic delight.

Cooley was in contact with Congressional leaders and state lawmakers who supported anti-bullying/hazing legislation. He was counting on these pending bills to be codified in federal or state statutes, creating zero tolerance for hazing and bullying.

Cooley was focusing much of his attention on Ohio after legislation entitled "Collin's Law" was codified in state statute. Collin Wiant, 18, died as a result of asphyxiation due to nitrous oxide in a hazing incident in 2018.

"Collin's Law" requires each public and private institution of higher education to adopt an anti-hazing policy.

Cooley wanted to build on 'Collin's Law" with stiffer criminal penalties at the federal level. Hazing through forced consumption of drugs and alcohol would be a second-degree felony punishable by a minimum mandatory five-year prison sentence.

But stronger criminal penalties were only part of the solution. Universities had been too permissive in policing and reporting incidents. That is why Cooley wanted federal funds to be withheld from universities that are incompliant with Title IX, the landmark federal law protecting students and university employees from discrimination based on sex and harassment.

Cooley often sounded like a broken record with this oft-repeated statement "We have to hit universities where it counts – in their deep pockets."

For his plan to make a difference, he instituted an anonymous hotline for victims to report threats of actual hazing. This was essential as only five percent of hazing incidents are reported to authorities because victims do not want to be rejected from the fraternity that they deem will fulfill their social life.

Cooley also knew his aversion for Greek Life was his ticket to ascend within the ranks of the DOJ. He wanted to strike when the iron was hot. This meant fixating on fraternities even though athletic teams, bands, and other clubs and groups at the high school and collegiate levels were also potential targets for hazing.

U.S. Attorney General Andrew Wadsworth had charged Cooley with heading a task force to gather data to determine the pervasiveness of out-of-control Greek Life. The U.S. attorney general contacted Cooley periodically to find out how the task force was progressing.

Cooley never forgot Wadsworth telling him that he is in a defining moment within his career -- a man in the right place at the right time.

Cooley knew there would be a bull's eye on his back in taking on the power, privilege, and influence associated with Greek Life.

In Cooley's mind, select fraternities were criminal enterprises inextricably linked to wealthy alumni with political connections and influence.

But Cooley had been assured by Wadsworth that the federal government would have his back when political pressure was brought to bear.

Cooley and Detective Lowry were proverbially joined at the hip. They relied on one another's cooperation.

But there was strife between the two men. Lowry had briefed Cooley about Trey and Mallory's public shaming. They agreed this incident had the makings of a mega media event with a young man and co-ed forced into a real-life walk of shame.

When pressed by Cooley, Detective Lowry was coy as to whether Trey and Mallory would cooperate as state witnesses,

"I believe you can take a horse to water and make it drink," Lowry said with a wink and nod.

Cooley looked downward, pausing as if he were amused by Lowry's comment. Then in one seamless motion, he glared into Lowry's eyes before speaking:

"Make no mistake, Trey and Mallory are victims and you are to treat them as such."

Cooley had no tolerance for Rambo tactics. He was a straight arrow and rules follower.

Cooley had assurance from State Attorney Davis that Trey and Mallory would not be prosecuted.

But Trey and Mallory were willing to meet with Detective Lowry and Deputy Brennan.

Detective Lowry played the bad cop; Deputy Brennan played the good cop. Lowry, his waist exhibiting a middle-aged paunch, wasted little time.

"So, Trey and Mallory, we want the people who took away your dignity and shamed each of you to pay for what they did," Detective Lowry said. "Deputy Brennan will take your full statement, and remember, we will need a full accounting – not just the ring leaders, but everyone involved," Detective Lowry said as if he were barking orders.

Mallory shifted in her chair. The thought of identifying Shelly as a suspect sent goosebumps down her spine. At this moment, she felt as if her spine was devoid of a backbone. She did not have the will to square off in a court of law against the likes of Shelly and her reviled sycophants.

Rather than acknowledging Mallory's fragility and gracefully allowing her to bow out as a prospective state witness, the detective double-downed, threatening her with prosecution.

"If you do not cooperate, we will be forced to charge you with public indecency," Lowry said. "If convicted, you would face a significant fine, community service, and probability of jail time."

Lowry ignored Trey. The detective knew Mallory was the linchpin for a case against Shelly, Hiriam, and the fraternity.

"Instill the fear of God in Mallory," Lowry told himself, "and a strong case will be made."

He asked her if she was prepared emotionally for jurors to view pictures of her and Trey in all their glory. Mallory interjected, "What are you talking about?"

With that question, Lowry knew he had Mallory's full attention. Lowry explained Mr. Arza's convenience store had surveillance cameras that videotaped all activity within the premises.

"There are several minutes of video footage of you and Trey entering and exiting the store," Lowry said.

The video, he said, has been parlayed into dozens of pictures. The detective leaned toward Mallory for full effect, pausing momentarily, then said:

"The pictures do not leave much to the imagination. If you are prosecuted, the prosecutor will offer the pictures as state evidence and disperse them to jurors."

Mallory covered her eyes as if she could eviscerate the images of her and Trey on full display for a prospective jury to peruse. Mallory's acumen or lack thereof for the criminal justice system was typical for an undergraduate college student.

Lowry was taking full advantage of her naivete and in doing so, she was easily manipulated and intimidated.

If legal counsel were at her disposal, she would have been advised Lowry does not render decisions in matters of prosecution. But more importantly, Lowry never would have had the opportunity to manipulate Mallory if she had retained an attorney. What Mallory did not know at this moment is State Attorney Davis would not prosecute her for public indecency because she was a victim of sexual assault.

There was irony in Lowry's attempted manipulation of Mallory. The detective wanted to elicit a statement from Mallory to incriminate Shelly, Hiram, and their accomplices. Yet, the detective was utilizing bullying tactics that would have made Shelly proud.

But at this moment, she refused to give Lowry what he wanted. His dubious tactics drew a sharp tone in her agitated voice:

"It is obvious you have no empathy for me. I am just another notch in your belt," Mallory said, mustering the fortitude to make eye contact with him. "I am going to talk to people who have my back."

Suddenly, Mallory was manifesting maturity beyond her years. She then asked, "Am I free to go?"

Lowry continued looking at the floor as if he were mesmerized by every nook and cranny within the non-carpeted surface, uttering, "You can leave, but do not go far."

While exiting the police station, Mallory was on the brink of tears.

Trey listened in silence as Mallory was on the verge of a meltdown, releasing pent-up emotions.

Mallory's voice escalated as she told Trey: "The detective is using us as pawns to get what he wants. My guess is he is all about arrests and convictions."

Mallory knew she had to come clean with her parents, but she was conflicted about asking Trey to accompany her. She knew Trey would be a willing ally and have her back, but his presence might exacerbate awkwardness with her parents.

This would be especially so, having her parents hear for the first time how she was stripped nude for coming to Trey's defense.

Mallory did not know whether her parents would affirm her for defending Trey or blame her and/or Trey for the depravity inflicted upon her. Mallory did not want to proceed alone. She decided there is strength in numbers.

Mallory reached out to Trey. Predictably, he acquiesced to her invitation. She packed a small suitcase, picked up Trey, and turned her car in the direction of I-10 East, heading for Savannah, Georgia, where her parents had resided since her birth 22 years ago.

She prepared herself mentally and emotionally to summarize the hazing event. As the only daughter of Sean and Patti O'Donnell, she knew an emotional breakdown in the throes of fragility and despair would crush her parents.

When she arrived at her parents' home in an upper-crust Savannah suburb, she was poised, or as much as she could be under the circumstances.

Her parents assumed Trey was her boyfriend, though Mallory introduced him as a "friend." During dinner, Patti intuitively sensed her daughter was troubled. Mallory could feel her mother's gaze through her Tortoise eyewear.

Patti, in her early 50s, looked like an older version of her daughter. They had the same interests too. When Mallory lived at home, they worked out at the local spa three mornings a week, then headed to Starbucks before shopping at boutique and antique shops.

It was not as if Mallory were telegraphing a hue and cry. However, her glow in which she could light up a room was conspicuously missing.

After dinner, Patti made a pot of freshly brewed coffee and suggested she, Sean, Mallory, and Trey transition to the backyard patio for further discussion. Or as Patti put it, to catch up.

Patti did not want to pressure Mallory into a knee-jerk cathartic response. She was hopeful a casual conversation would allow her daughter to segue into whatever she wanted to share.

Mallory eventually laid the predicate for her sordid state of affairs by saying, "Mom and Dad, I have something to tell you."

Sean and Patti were bracing for news of an engagement, though they believed Mallory was too young for marriage.

Sean's and Patti's eyes fixated on Mallory, then they glanced at Trey, who was expressionless. Mallory attempted to be detached emotionally as she laid out the sordid events.

She knew anything less than a stoic disposition would fuel her parents' reaction, particularly Sean's.

Despite Mallory's best efforts, Sean's and Patti's blood began to boil as they envisioned their daughter publicly humiliated and then threatened with a jury trial to be victimized again. While looking at Trey with a hint of judgment in his eyes, Sean interjected, with indignation in his voice, then added:

"Mallory, I assume you want the people who committed these acts against you to pay for their crimes?"

Mallory knew her father like a book. He was fire and brimstone. In his mind, there is right and wrong and no gray in between.

Prepared for her father's question, Mallory paused, then responded in her rehearsed narrative: "There is a part of me that wants justice, but justice comes with a price."

Her voice went silent before she mustered courage for a confrontational comment: "You do not know the people responsible for this as I do. "They are sociopaths who come from wealthy families."

Patti then asked, "Ok Mallory, we hear you. What do you want?"

Before Mallory answered, Sean placed his hand above his head as if he were a traffic cop holding a stop sign.

"I need you to stop, Mallory. Your mother and I are hearing this for the first time and candidly, it is difficult to absorb."

Patti, sitting next to Sean, stepped on her husband's foot for him to desist. But Sean did not heed his wife's not-so-subtle gesture. He then glared at Trey with his penetrating green eyes, then summarily dismissed him from the patio in which he was instructed to wait in the foyer, well beyond earshot of the conversation.

Mallory protested, "Dad, that was rude. I invited Trey to be here for me."

Under the circumstances, Sean could be forgiven for unabashedly sowing discord.

Sean asked for her daughter's understanding, then asked, "Mallory, I need to know if Trey attempted to defend you."

She then recounted that Trey did all he could do under the circumstances.

Sean was less than satisfied with his daughter's explanation. He was directing his anger at Trey, who was a convenient target.

Patti sensed this, then added as she grabbed her husband's hand, "I know you are furious. I am too. But the young man in the foyer is not the problem."

Mallory, attempting to redirect the conversation, said, "Mom and Dad, what I want is an exit strategy."

Sean clutched his daughter's hand, conveying his best mea culpa: "I know my reaction was less than desirable. Your mother and I love you more than you know.

"It makes perfect sense that you would come to us. You are not alone. We are in this together," Sean said.

Sean and Patti asked Mallory to stay the night, but she politely begged off, citing her burgeoning class schedule. That was only part of the truth. She did not know whether Trey would be invited as an overnight guest.

Moreover, as They stood awkwardly alone in the foyer, Mallory did not know if he would accept such an invitation Moments after Mallory and Trey departed, Sean contacted a well-known criminal defense attorney in Savannah, Bart McIntosh. Within days, McIntosh contacted Cooley about Lowry's threat to prosecute Trey and Mallory for public indecency.

Cooley assured McIntosh no charges would be filed.

A seething Cooley contacted an unapologetic Lowry. "You have no authority over the Leon County Sheriff's Office," a smug Lowry told Cooley.

Cooley's next move was to contact Leon County Sheriff Roy Hill and State Attorney Davis.

Sheriff Hill equivocated, refusing to undermine his hard-charging detective.

"I'll have to get back to you," Sheriff Hill told Cooley. The sheriff was buying time to talk with Lowry before responding to Cooley.

But internally, the sheriff was furious Lowry poured gas on a fire that never should have been ignited. But Lowry was persuasive when talking with Sheriff Hill: "Forget about Cooley and the feds. This is our town and there is another hazing incident right in our backyard. By placing pressure on the two victims, we can get to those who are criminally responsible."

Sheriff Hill did not disagree with Detective Lowry's strategic vision to use Trey and Mallory to get to the real criminals.

Sheriff Hill told Lowry to undertake no action until he talks with State Attorney Davis.

"That is an order," the sheriff said, making eye contact with the detective. Lowry, knowing Davis would not prosecute Trey and Mallory, defied the sheriff's orders. He had Trey and Mallory arrested with public indecency, hoping they would incriminate the fraternity and sorority members responsible for the hazing in exchange for the charges being dropped.

There was a chain reaction once Mallory was charged. She called her dad, who called Attorney McIntosh, who called State Attorney Davis. The State Attorney assured McIntosh that a "no bill" would be expeditiously filed, stating there is insufficient evidence for the case to move forward.

But Trey and Mallory received a court notice for them to attend an arraignment hearing while the charges were pending. The hearing was brief in which Attorney McIntosh stated "not guilty" in response to the charges.

There were whispers that a journalist with the Tallahassee Democrat would be attending the hearing.

But fortunately for Trey and Mallory, no media coverage promulgated their public shaming. Lowry had played his last card and lost. He had no leverage to coerce Trey and Mallory to testify as state witnesses. Within hours after the arraignment, Trey and Mallory had the "no bill" in hand and could breathe a sigh of relief.

Chapter 8

Straw that Broke the Camel's Back

Trey had survived two horrific incidents without seriously contemplating suicide. But a third public shaming would be akin to the straw that broke the camel's back.

Thomas and Katharine wanted to know what provoked Trey to jump from the Skyway Bridge. The Barrys decided to hire a private investigator, Bruce Gronkowski, a straight-talking no-nonsense detective, to investigate Trey's life in the weeks leading up to his attempted suicide.

Bruce was like a dog with a bone: give him a job and come hell or high water, he will see it to the end. He went about his work with unbridled attention, leaving no tangential stone unturned. He was an old-school detective, eliciting information from persons of interest and their families and friends. He also was adapting to technology as a middle-aged man, wisely allowing the Internet to do his leg work by using spyware and tapping into websites that elicit criminal background checks, financial records, past and present residencies, and relevant commentary on social media platforms.

Bruce, who relinquished his badge under suspicious circumstances, was well known within the south-side community of St. Petersburg.

Bruce, bombastic and cacophonic, was bigger than life. His persona manifested bravado and swagger. He demanded attention and metaphorically consumed oxygen from any room he occupied. His deep-resounding voice was intimidating for anyone who was on the receiving end of his questions.

Bruce also was predictable to a fault, cozying up at local watering holes and visiting Skyway Jacks for breakfast nearly every morning.

Bruce's first order of business was to contact state legislator John Connolly, who had agreed as a family friend of the Barrys, to oversee an internship for Trey.

Rep. Connolly, who maintained a chiseled physique by working out at a gym only minutes from the State Capital, was well aware Trey was a fragile young man who needed positive reinforcement to place him on an upward trajectory.

Rep. Connolly assured Thomas that Trey would be mentored under his direct supervision. Trey, however, was not looking forward to the Internship. He had no personal issue with Rep. Connolly or any other legislator.

At that time, Thomas and Katharine were hopeful that under Rep. Connolly's tutelage, Trey would hone skills to boost his confidence to jump-start a career within state government. The internship seemed like a good idea at that time for Trey to use his fifth year as an undergraduate to complete his Bachelor of Political Science degree and obtain invaluable professional experience.

Trey had to retake several classes due to poor grades and had never earned more than 13 hours of credit in a semester, which explained why he needed a fifth year to earn his undergraduate degree.

Rep. Connolly was altruistically driven. He was convinced Trey was much like many young people who simply needed a confidence boost for them to have direction in their professional lives.

Rep. Connolly had been inspired by his life's experiences as a somewhat floundering young man who found his niche in public policy under the direction of a policy wonk for a not-for-profit organization. He was further motivated to assist Trey based on Edward D. Hale's writings. Hale was a nineteenth-century author and clergyman.

One of Hale's quotes particularly resonated with Rep. Connolly: "I am only one, but still I am one, and I cannot do everything, but still I can do something. And, because I cannot do everything, I will not refuse to do something that I can do."

Rep. Connolly was so moved by Hale's quote, he inscribed it on a piece of paper tucked in his billfold. Each time he opened the wallet, he would see the note, constantly reminding him to not refuse what he can do.

But Rep. Connolly wrongfully assumed Trey majored in political science because he had an affinity for public policy.

For Trey, selecting a major was driven by a path of least resistance. Political science was far less challenging than pursuing a degree in hard sciences.

He would not have given political science a second thought if he had the self-confidence to pass the prerequisites – biology, calculus, and physics – to pursue a degree in marine science, which was his true passion.

There was an irony of sorts in which he spurned the opportunity to follow his passion to study marine life while opting for a major that induced nothing more than apathy.

Trey was a minimalist, unmotivated to do little more than show up for classes. His apathetic approach stemmed in part from his parents' oft-repeated exhortations to view politics through a critical lens.

Trey was as apolitical as anyone. He viewed politics as nefarious and politicians as Machiavellian, but a necessary evil in a representative democracy. His cynical pragmatism convinced him investing time and energy in the public policy arena had more to do with supporting party politics and partisan agendas than effectuating policies for the common good.

His presumption that the Legislature's ambiance was caustic and polarizing sent a chill down his spine.

As a political neophyte interning for Rep. Connolly, Trey was unprepared for a daily dose of vitriolic rhetoric and political power plays in which beltway insiders cloaked their political agendas in the name of public good to get what they wanted.

Trey was initially in disbelief at how lobbyists and other special interest groups could be so two-faced, manifesting congeniality on the surface, then playing high-stakes politics in back rooms with a take-no-prisoners approach.

In Trey's mind, one day in the cutthroat world of high-powered politics was one day too many.

But despite Trey's antipathy for politics, he was the quintessential obedient son, agreeing to the internship at the behest of his parents.

Thomas and Katharine were convinced Trey would blossom personally and professionally under the watchful eyes of Rep. Connolly.

Rep. Connolly believed Trey could meet this challenge head-on and in doing so, reinforce a positive self image.

In Rep. Connolly's mind, his bill – a pathway for non-traditional students to obtain work skills through career track – was the perfect legislative vehicle for Trey to publicly testify before the House Education Committee.

But Rep. Connolly was not aware Trey avoided public speaking as if were the plague. Stammering and stuttering were embedded in his memory as a high school student presenting a book report.

In a meeting with Rep. Connolly, Bruce pursed his lips as he envisioned Trey not wanting to disappoint his parents, but bewildered at the prospect of public speaking.

"Look, I was hoping Trey would develop a bit of swagger and bounce in his step to transition from self-effacing and deprecating," Rep. Connolly told Bruce.

But Rep. Connolly turned away, refusing to make eye contact with Bruce before finding his voice again.

I was advised by my legislative aide, Bryce Underwood, that Trey had a self-inflicted meltdown.

"I was convinced Trey needed an opportunity to be propped up to have his moment in which he would begin to transition from shy and self-effacing to a confident young man," Rep. Connolly said.

Bruce asked Rep. Connelly if he could interview his staff.

"Absolutely yes," Rep. Conolly answered, then added he had assigned Bryce to assist in Trey's preparation for the testimony.

"If anyone on my staff can shed light as to what transpired, Bryce would be that person," Rep. Connolly emphatically said. "Bryce can be available at your earliest convenience."

Bruce's intuitive senses, backed by more than 30 years of law enforcement experience, told him to circumvent Bryce by interviewing others about Bryce's relationship with Trey.

In Bruce's thought process, Bryce was not a person of interest.

"Hell," Bruce bemused, "there was no reason to believe crimes have been committed."

Bruce was bent on following evidence instead of targeting Bryce. His strategy was to interview all legislative aides, interns, and volunteers whose paths intersected with Trey.

In Bruce's mind, this process would eventually eliminate or implicate Bryce.

In the ensuing days ahead, Bruce interviewed Stephen York and Julie Dixon, who were legislative aides for Josh Noble, vice chair of the House Education Committee.

Julie and Stephen worked closely with Bryce and Rep. Connolly's office. Rep. Connolly was chair of the House Education Committee.

Stephen looked like the boy next door with short blond cropped hair, and an athletic build on his six-foot, two-inch frame.

Julie, a petite brunette with short coiffed hair and luminous pale white skin, was the spitting image of the prototypical legal secretary, especially when she was bespectacled with her dark-framed glasses.

Raised in a working poor family in South Georgia, Julie wanted to live a good life. She would do whatever necessary to be ensconced in material wealth.

In scheduled interviews with Bruce, Julie, and Stephen were poised and cooperative. They had answers to every question.

For Bruce, this was a bit of a red flag. Julie and Stephen may have been too good in their interviews.

But soon thereafter, Bruce obtained a treasure trove of information from one of Bryce's former girlfriends, Lauren Palluda. Lauren was a woman scorned, and she cathartically spilled Bryce's dirty laundry. She described her ex as a philanderer of dalliance proportion.

Most importantly for Bruce, Lauren claimed Bryce had confided in her about his diabolical plot to undermine Rep. Connolly and publicly humiliate Trey.

Lauren not only described Bryce as the mastermind of his conspiratorial scheme but provided detailed accounts of how he morphed into the worst version of himself.

Bruce was impressed with Lauren's attention to detail and candor, which did not always portray herself in a positive light.

One such example was Lauren reflecting on Bryce's revenge when he was denied a promotion.

"Revenge," she said, "comes from a dark place within."

Bruce wondered whether she was referring to Bryce's revenge or her revenge on him.

The irony was not lost on Bruce that Lauren was seeking revenge as a woman scorned.

As Lauren sipped on her vanilla latte at Skyway Jacks, Bruce set his handheld tape recorder to play and asked her to start from the beginning.

Lauren nodded her head, cleared her throat, and said, "Bryce could be ingratiatingly polite by turning on the charm to get what he wanted."

But she said Bryce could turn hot or cold in a New York second.

"More times than not, Bryce was mercurial as if he were a chameleon, morphing from brief moments of emotional highs, to aloof and introverted, to extreme lows," she said.

Bruce pressed Lauren about Bryce having vices other than infidelity that would further explain his mood swings.

"Bryce was not addicted to drugs and alcohol, but he had an insatiable appetite for control and power," Lauren said. "It was as if control in his domain was his drug of choice."

Bryce's obsession with authority and his seemingly dead-end job was a hellish combination, Lauren said.

Lauren added that although Bryce perceived himself as Machiavellian, he was reputed for having an aversion to detail. She said those who worked closely with him knew his knowledge was superficially a foot long and an inch deep.

Suffice to say, Bryce's skill set was not replete with requisite skills and his work was mediocre at best, she said.

"It was as if he were in a distracted state of mind," Lauren said, refusing to expound on distractions related to his infidelity.

Lauren dabbed at her eyes with a hand-wrenched tissue while suggesting Bryce wanted Rep. Connolly to pull political strings for him to be promoted as staff director of the House Education Committee.

But Rep. Connolly did not believe Bryce was ready to ascend, Lauren said, because Bryce was not a good fit for policy work.

And Bryce, Lauren said, alienated legislative staff and constituents with his uneven temperament.

Lauren said when Rep. Connolly refused to promote Bryce, he copped a bilious attitude as he continued to receive the same salary in the position for which he was hired.

Lauren paused as Bruce awaited details. She then dropped a bombshell by explaining;

Bryce's disposition further soured when Rep. Connolly announced Trey would be presenting sponsored testimony before the House Education Committee. He took umbrage that Rep. Connolly had chosen a lowly intern to deliver testimony. In Bryce's mind, that responsibility should have been delegated to him as the trusted senior legislative aide.

Lauren said Bryce was hell-bent on retribution.

Lauren's professional position as a librarian, not a clinician, did not impede her from defining Bryce's behavior as "twisted" and evaluating him as a sociopath, paranoid schizophrenic, and habitual liar.

"Bryce was Dr. Jekyll and Mr. Hyde while possessing a false sense of reality," Lauren said, as he diabolically plotted against anyone whom he believed stood in his way for what he deemed was rightfully his.

Lauren then leaned over the table, her brown eyes unflinching as she spoke in a soft but emphatic voice only for him to hear:

"It was this demented mindset for him to be the survivor of the fittest in which he gave no quarter to adversaries. It was either them or him, conquer or be conquered."

Bruce then asked her about steps Bryce undertook to garner his pound of flesh.

Bryce's first order of business, she said, was ensuring Rep. Connolly's bill was on the committee agenda for sponsored testimony.

Bryce convinced Rep. Connolly to concoct an out-of-state obligation why he could neither be at the State Capital, nor in the Sunshine State, on the day Trey presented testimony.

Lauren said Bryce recruited two legislative aides for the plot to be carried out.

Bruce interjected: "Were the aides Stephen York and Julie Dixon?"

Lauren responded, "That rings a bell, but I am not sure."

Lauren said Bryce did not share details about the plot.

Bruce would have to rely on someone other than Lauren for the rest of the story.

Bruce was connecting the dots. If Bryce threw women under the bus, then he could certainly do so with an easy mark such as Trey.

For Bruce, Lauren's candor could be the break in the case to catch Bryce in a web of deceit.

Bruce would have to verify Lauren's version of the truth as she had a vested interest to portray Bryce in the least favorable light.

Bruce had no immediate recourse than to turn to Trey, whose recollection of the developments leading up to the public testimony was a work in progress.

Initially, Trey did not know about what had transpired. But Bruce contacted Fr. Liam, who engaged Trey in several sessions to help induce his memory.

Trey's recall improved and his repressed feelings about Bryce were manifesting.

"Bryce is a despot at this inner core regardless of his attempts to mask his evil spirit," Trey said with invective condemnation.

Trey said Bryce held court with his proteges, Julie and Stephen, venting his frustrations about anyone who disagreed with him.

"Bryce could be shrewd," Trey said, "but more times than not, he was just loud and overbearing."

As Trey continued, his anger exacerbated into a venomous rage in a self-proclaimed script for retribution.

Bruce interjected, asking Trey about other witnesses who overheard Bryce's diatribes.

Trey paused pensively, contemplating there should be no shortage of witnesses who were aware of Bryce's exploits. He grinned from ear to ear as if he had an epiphany declaring: "Rep. Noble's legislative aide, Victor Rosen, was chummy with Bryce, Julie, and Stephen."

Bruce wasted no time contacting Victor.

Bruce quickly discovered Victor was an impressive witness. He was not complicit with Bryce but had a bird's eye view of Bryce careening out of control in his conspiratorial plot.

Victor recounted Bryce routinely met with Julie and Stephen under the guise of providing materials for upcoming House Education Committee meetings.

Bryce would portray himself as a victim, Victor said, then revel in delight in how to plot his revenge.

"Bryce was striking a chord with Julie and Stephen," Victor said.

On one occasion, Victor said he overheard Bryce appealing to Julie's and Stephen's emotions.

"Place yourselves in my shoes by imagining your legislator circumventing you to delegate a high-profile responsibility to a neophyte," Victor quoted Bryce as saying.

Victor said Bryce asserted: "You would be right to ask why your legislator has so little confidence in you."

Victor said Bryce's commentary distorted reality by ignoring the fact Rep. Connolly's decision was not an indictment of Bryce, but an opportunity for Trey to springboard his confidence to ascend from the ranks of mediocrity.

Victor, a practicing Lutheran, said Bryce would have understood Rep. Connolly's intentions if he were well versed in the New Testament in which a landowner paid men whom he hired in the afternoon the same wage as men who were hired in the morning.

Victor expounded as if he were reciting excerpts from the Sermon on the Mount: "The men who worked a full day received wages that were agreed upon. They were treated fairly, much like Bryce. But the men who were hired in the early morning were angry they did not receive a higher wage than the men hired in the afternoon.

Rep. Connolly's altruistic attempt to instill confidence in Trey had nothing to do with Bryce, who continued receiving the same salary in the same position for which he was hired."

But in Bryce's mind, he was the victim of Rep. Connolly reaching out to Trey, Victor said.

"It did not matter that Bryce's conspiracy theories were akin to building a house of cards devoid of a foundation," Victor said.

"In Bryce's depraved mind, an oft-repeated conspiracy theory or unadulterated lie eventually is believable," Victor said. "Like so many sociopaths, Bryce possessed the beguiling of an accomplished con artist."

Victor's words meshed with Bruce's real-world experiences of con artists who repeat a falsehood with such fervor that it is eventually accepted as the Gospel Truth.

There was no doubt that Bryce's manipulative prowess struck a chord with Stephen and Julie, Victor said. The trio, he said, were on their way as conspirators to be saboteurs in a confluence of repugnancy.

Victor was pulling no punches as he recalled Bryce's sinister and incredibly subversive plot.

"It all but guaranteed a public spectacle such that Rep. Connolly's judgment would be scrutinized," Victor said.

Victor described Stephen and Julie as sycophants, heeding Bryce's directives as if he were a master stratagem in a high-stakes game of power and manipulation.

But according to Victor, Bryce, Julie, and Stephen shared the common bond of treachery in which they were willing to have their version of a coup d' etat to discourage any legislator from elevating an intern to a high-profile assignment.

Victor recalled overhearing Bryce boasting that pulling the wool over Trey's eyes was too easy.

"As Bryce reveled in insidious subterfuge, his eyes twinkled with sheer delight as he flashed a devilish grin," Victor said.

Victor said Bryce was Trey's, Judas Iscariot. Bryce, Victor said. gave Trey a hardy handshake and offered him encouraging words on the day that the testimony was to be presented. Bryce invaded Trey's personal space by straightening his tie, quipping;

"If you look good, you will deliver."

Victor became emotional, clenching his fists as he recalled Julie and Stephen descending upon Trey, who was seated in the committee room.

Victor said a smiling Julie playfully jabbed at Trey's shoulders, punctuating the moment with a wink as she asked him to join her outside of the committee room.

Victor said Trey appeared reluctant to heed her request, but Julie would not take no for an answer.

Victor overheard Julie's exhortation "Don't worry, Trey. "I just need a moment of your time."

Trey followed Julie, leaving his testimony in a three-ring binder on the bench where he had been seated.

Victor said he observed Stephen opening the binder and extracting several pages.

"It became obvious those pages were Trey's testimony," Victor said. "Once Stephen had what he needed, he walked by Trey and Julie.

"At that moment," Victor said, "Julie's mood was suddenly cold and detached,"

Victor said Trey returned to his seat in the committee room, anxiously thumbing through the notebook for his testimony. He was frantic, Victor said, as beads of sweat permeated his forehead while his eyes presumably were telling his brain the talking points had vanished. With this realization, Victor said Trey was in full panic mode. His hands began to shake uncontrollably as if had Parkinson's Disease.

With the talking points, Trey would have predictably read the text verbatim, completing the presentation with a modicum of professionalism.

Absent the script, he would be a lost soul, reduced to utter incoherence on a public platform as if he lacked the mental acuity to articulate.

One by one, witnesses were summoned to the podium as if they were in a queue.

Trey was next in line.

As Trey waited in torment, Victor said he had a look of a deer in the headlights.

From that point onward, Bruce relied on the Florida Channel's videotaped telecast. Although Victor's and Lauren's recollections were helpful, there is no substitute for videotape. It is what it is.

Bruce watched the tape as Vice Chair Noble, substituting for Chair Connolly, summoned for Trey to present testimony.

Bryce stood, approached Trey and put his arm around his shoulder, and responded to the chair:

"The witness is having some difficulties. Can you give us a few moments?"

Vice Chair Noble then granted a brief recess as Bryce feigned a display of sincerity, masking his deceit as he worked the room with the fluidity of a charismatic and eloquent schmoozer.

Bryce had set the table for Trey's public humiliation.

Trey's life was flashing before his eyes. His impending testimony would be a horrendous spectacle, indelibly shaming him.

Bruce detected Trey was on such mental overload that he was mimicking manifestations of a nervous breakdown.

"It was almost as if Trey were in a scene from Scanners when a character's head combusted," Bruce told himself.

Bryce's voice was audible as he beseeched Trey:

"What are you doing?" Be a man and walk up to the podium and give your best shot."

Trey looked at Bryce and began to dribble in utterance.

But Bryce slapped Trey on his shoulder, nudging him toward the podium.

Trey's legs were so weak that he wobbled in his walk of shame to address the committee.

Trey hoped for gravitas, but there was none among the triumvirate of Bryce, Julie, and Stephen.

A peculiar dispassionate gaze fell on Trey. He intermittently squinted his eyes as if he were in myopia and his mind was telling him that this moment of living hell was real.

The veins on Trey's forehead vexed, manifesting mental anguish.

He had no audible words, nor coherent thoughts.

The audience's reaction was typical of cultural incivility and insensitivity. Most of the attendees gaped and sneered at him. A few snickered and even appeared to revel in Trey's shame.

But two middle-aged women placed their hands over their mouths to muffle their gasps. They awkwardly looked away, unable to watch Trey's mortification.

As a big belly security officer escorted Trey from the podium, light bulbs flashed and cameras clicked from the Capitol Press Corp. The scene was almost surreal as if it were a primordial rendition of Romans feeding Christians to lions.

There was little doubt Trey's shaming was a sacrifice of monumental proportion as his public image and life would change.

In his catatonic state, Trey did not feel mortified at the moment. He was tone-deaf and detached from reality.

He was, however, emotionally emasculated.

His body was listless as his energy level was depleted to the core.

Chapter 9

Trey's Planned Demise

In the ensuing weeks, Trey was in the throes of deep-seated despair. He had no sense of hope and will to live. His severe depression placed him in a downward spiral preparing him for the end.

And his public shaming continued. The maw of social media was scathing. Blogs reporting on Trey's breakdown were ruthless, impugning Trey's intelligence with labels that would not be tolerated if directed at anyone with a documented cognitive disability.

One report condemned the Pinellas County School System for allowing Trey to graduate from high school. Another report rebuked the University of Pensacola-Tallahassee for granting Trey admission to the university.

To cope, Trey withdrew from reality, living as if he were in a cocoon, refusing to reach out to his parents, siblings, and Rep. Connolly.

Initially, he had no memory of the confluence of repugnancy from Bryce, Julie, and Stephen. To suggest he was in a deep moronic state would be an understatement.

For Trey, living in this hellish world was worse than death. He secretly wished to be put down, like a suffering animal.

But no one, not even Bryce, was willing to deliver a coup de grace.

If Trey's life were to suddenly end, he would have to take matters into his own hands.

Although Trey was not a victim of rape, he could identify with female victims who are tried in the court of public opinion as reprehensible for the acts committed upon them.

In at least one respect, Trey was undergoing his version of "slut shaming" – a colloquialism to describe young women who are victims of drug-induced sexual assault in which their classmates turn on them.

In Trey's case, he too was falsely branded. He had to own a narrative that he had no one else to blame but himself because he was unprepared, incompetent, and unqualified to speak before a legislative committee. He philosophically pondered that no one should be judged solely on his or her worst day.

Trey realized society is predicated on unmercifully tearing down people, especially if they cannot defend themselves

Like so many times in his young life, Trey had been given short shrift, feeling alone as if he did not belong among the living.

He was in a state of hopelessness and at his nadir, beaten into utter submission. He had neither the will nor the energy to move forward.

This was new territory for Trey. Although he had been bullied and shamed at various times in his life, he did not have a history of manic depression.

Heretofore, he had no protracted fixation with taking his life. But the thought of doing the unthinkable was now on the table for consideration. He was so empty – emotionally, mentally, and physically.

There was something else. It was too painful to live under the fear that perpetrated evil would revisit him.

It was then that he set out to end his misery, forever.

In short order, Trey returned to St. Petersburg but did so without the knowledge of his family.

He drove his Volkswagen to Bill Jackson's Sporting Goods on 34th Street where he purchased a pup tent, lantern, and a few other camping accessories.

His next order of business was to purchase a few snacks and hard liquor. With Irish blood running through his veins, Trey wanted the burn of 90-proof Jameson Whiskey making its way down his pallet to dull the realization of what he was planning to do.

Trey then headed to the Fort DeSoto Campground, where he pitched his tent and ingested the whiskey straight up for it to have a bitter taste in a good sort of way.

But if there were any hope of an internal battle in Trey's conscience about his death wish, it was dashed when he imbibed the whiskey as a depressant fueling his morose.

Trey fell asleep in a stupor. When he awakened, he was convinced this very day would be his very last. He was, however, unsettled about descending to his death in the Gulf waters and possibly ravaged by sharks.

Trey was at peace jumping from the Skyway as a means to end his life, but the thought of being torn apart from a man-eating predator was terrifying.

In Trey's mind, committing suicide was not a masochistic act. He wanted to die devoid of a tortuous ending.

Trey's fear was alleviated when he realized the chance of being attacked by a shark was about the same as being struck by lightning.

And, he was further comforted by the thought that the fall from the Skyway would instantly kill him. If he were to be attacked by a shark, it likely would be in a posthumous state.

That thought reminded Trey of the movie—Butch Cassidy and the Sundance Kid—in which Paul Newman (Butch Cassidy) and Robert Redford (Sundance) were vacillating about whether to jump from a cliff into a river as Bolivian vigilantes attempted to capture them.

Sundance tells Butch he can't swim. Butch responded, "Hell, the fall will kill you."

Although the lines from the movie were pure fiction, Trey perceived them as an eureka moment. A shark attack and the incapability of swimming in a river were irrelevant if there were an instant death.

Trey was convinced his neck would be immediately broken when crashing into the sea.

There was one other task for Trey before driving to the Skyway. He composed a letter for his parents. It stated:

Dear Mom and Dad:

When you read this, I shall no longer be on this Earth. Please do not blame yourselves. I was blessed to have each of you as loving parents. But living was simply too hard. I no longer have the strength to withstand evil in this world. Please pray for my reposed soul. Your loving son,

Trey

Writing the letter reminded Trey of a lecture he attended as a high school student at Ellis Island in which a professor of international studies at Columbia University said no other people endured more dire challenges than 18th century Irish, who were beset with the potato famine and then not recognized as human by the British Crown.

Trey's eyes welled as he choked back sobs while sealing the note in an envelope and placing it on the dashboard of his car. He then composed himself before driving the car to his anticipated destiny of death.

Trey was relieved no vehicles were in sight when he stopped his car on the center span. He wanted to control his anticipated final hour without any outside interference.

He got his wish, or so it seemed. His plan to end his life was unencumbered.

Days later, Trey lay on a hospital bed, contemplating his life from tortured soul to seeking suicide, to the pronouncement of being clinically dead and now a newfound survivor.

Trey asked himself whether he could ascend from the ashes of despair and a new beginning.

The answer to his question was clear as mud. He was damaged goods, but his parents, siblings, and Fr. Liam were hell-bent on giving him a second chance.

Chapter 10

Risky Business

There may be optimism for a healthy recovery from one horrendously tormenting episode. A second nightmarish episode would blight that optimism. A third-type episode would be foreboding.

The possibility of Trey assimilating into society as a healthy-well adjusted person appeared to be slim and none.

As Thomas, Katharine, and Fr. Liam pondered Trey's recovery, they reviewed literature from a Dr. Phil-type wilderness program in Ashtabula, Ohio.

The program was established to extricate patients from a problematic environment and replace it with an inner circle of therapists, counselors, and spiritual advisors in a natural habitat.

Fr. Liam was a strong proponent of wilderness programs, having served as a spiritual advisor at a Dallas-based program.

Thomas and Katharine rubber-stamped Fr. Liam's recommendations for Trey to participate in the Ohio-based wilderness program.

There was consensus with Trey's acquiescence.

In the immediate days ahead, Trey completed the protocols associated with brain trauma from his concussion and was released from St. Petersburg General Hospital.

Trey returned to his parents' home for a week, fishing, boating, and soul-searching while enjoying long walks on Suncoast beaches. Then, Trey and Fr. Liam boarded a flight from Tampa to Youngstown, where they were greeted by the program's clinical psychologist, Gerald Faith.

Gerald, a slender, introverted man, chauffeured Trey and Fr. Liam to the Wilderness Program. Aside from an initial greeting from Gerald, he uttered nary a word while making the 50-mile trek to the Wilderness Program.

Gerald was not antithetical to conversation. He could talk when conversing with his peers or meeting with philanthropists interested in his research.

But the quintessential Gerald was in his element at a cubicle reviewing profiles of patients with psychological disorders.

For the most part, Gerald's geekiness was not a problem. He rarely was in the spotlight. When he was required to lead a discussion, he used such cliches as – "It is not over until it is over, it is what it is" and his favorite, "If it quacks like a duck, walks like a duck, it must be a duck."

But he awkwardly spewed these cliches as if he were extemporaneously commenting on cue when in actuality they were perceived by audiences as prescribed.

He was stale and robotic. This was abundantly clear when subjects bared their souls about life-changing events such as drug, alcohol, and domestic abuse, and Gerald typically responded with thank you for sharing, followed by awkward silence.

He was not uncaring and insensitive. He simply did not possess the social etiquette for any level of ingratiation.

As Gerald's white Ford SUV headed on a coastal road parallel to Lake Eric, Trey wondered whether the ambiance was similar to the Florida Suncoast.

He soon discovered that although Ashtabula was aesthetically beautiful, it was not a tourist destination.

Few traveled to Ashtabula for gravitas.

They arrived at a large, austere-looking cabin. Gerald escorted Trey and Fr. Liam through an entrance that only an avid hunter would appreciate. Moose and deer heads were mounted on walls, prompting Fr Liam to opine:

"At one point or another, this building must have been a hunting lodge."

Trey, out of character, responded, "Thank you for the comment, Captain Obvious."

Then Trey, finding his bearings as an animal rights advocate and supporter of People for the Ethical Treatment of Animals (PETA), asked whether a vegan menu would be available for dinner.

Fr. Liam did not respond, refusing to take the bait. But Fr. Liam was amused and encouraged Trey may be undertaking initial steps to assert his opinion, albeit with a sense of humor.

Gerald walked to the door of a dormitory room, unlocked it, and quietly spoke to no one in particular:

'Our accommodations do not have much in the way of amenities, but are comfortable and should meet your needs."

Fr. Liam added, sounding paternal, "Trey, wash up for dinner and bring your IPAD. There will be an orientation later in the evening."

Before dinner, Fr. Liam positioned himself at center stage, asking those gathered to stand and bow their heads, placing themselves in the presence of the Lord by giving thanks for the Wilderness Program and the bountiful food before them.

Not everyone stood. A couple of attendees conversed in what was supposed to be silent mediation. This uncooperativeness may have had more to do with the behavioral and emotional challenges of several attendees than outright obstinance of faith.

Fr. Liam intentionally positioned himself at a table with therapists, counselors, coaches, and trainers. He wanted to give Trey space to socialize with fellow attendees.

Trey knew how to break the ice to stimulate small talk with strangers, even in the aftermath of his victimization of public shaming, bullying, and attempted suicide.

But two young men seated at Trey's table were reclusive. Mitch Hatcher, a Gothic-looking 19-year-old, scarcely made eye contact with anyone. He mostly looked across the table to no one in particular in inexplicable voyeuristic delight as his eyes blinked involuntarily.

Mitch, with a fork and knife in each hand, cut a six-inch sirloin steak with the precision of a doctor's scaffold.

The other introvert, Dexter Martin, could have been Mitch's twin brother. Dexter was perceptive and intuitive. He sensed Trey was somewhat amused with Mitch.

"Mitch is on the pervasive spectrum for Autism and is bipolar too," Dexter said, bluntly talking about Mitch in his presence.

Dexter neither had a filter, nor social graces. He spewed whatever flashed through his mind.

Following dinner, a burly, chiseled middle-aged man rang a bell. All eyes focused on the man with the bell in hand.

"Greetings gentleman. My name is Coach Rassas. My job over the next few weeks is to toughen each of you up.

"But we are going to have a good time doing it," he said, faintly smiling as his dark-brown eyes gazed at the audience.

Coach Rassas introduced Gerald, Fr. Liam, and Dr. Richard Synder, a psychiatrist, and director of the Wilderness Program.

Dr. Synder portrayed himself as an open-minded, forward-thinking progressive who was fond of saying decisions should be driven by science. He was speaking within the context of hard sciences in the study of the human brain and social sciences within the construct of human behavior.

But his outward manifestation of open-mindedness belied an inner self of intolerance, arrogance, and ill-temperedness.

He looked the part of the prototypical professor with thick-framed glasses and slicked-back dark hair. More often than not, his attire included an unbuttoned Polo sweater and a tobacco pipe in hand. The pipe was more of a prop than anything else.

There were whispers that the pipe more often than not was tobacco-less. He was known to remove the pipe from his mouth and point it as if to punctuate a particular emphasis while in serious discourse.

In some respects, he was a case study in role-playing the suave, intellectual mental health expert.

Truth be known, Dr. Synder's behavior was consistent with self-idolatry. He was reputed for self-promotion to the detriment of his colleagues.

Compliments and affirmations on his behalf were in short supply. Moreover, he had a short fuse in which his repressed anger would boil over into acrimony. When this occurred, Dr. Synder was in a raw state of emotion, not much different than some of his clients.

Dr. Synder's distractors accused him of hypocrisy, claiming he rejected science when it did not jive with his views, such as supporting a woman's right to choose abortion even within there is incontrovertible scientific evidence that an unborn child met the viability test to live outside the womb.

At the initial dinner for Trey and the other attendees, Dr. Synder conveyed a unifying message.

Coach Rassas briefly reviewed the program's handbook. In a husky stentorian voice, he proclaimed alcoholic beverages and drugs were prohibited, except for authorized prescriptions approved by the program's medical staff in consultation with attendees' physicians.

"Violations of these rules," Coach Rassas said, "will result in expulsion from the program. No exceptions."

Before adjourning the meeting, Coach Rassas announced attendees to go to their rooms and turn off lights within 15 minutes.

"Rest well," Coach Rassas said, "because your day begins at dawn with a 10-mile hike."

As Trey headed to his room, he wondered if the Wilderness Program was a synonym for a boot camp and whether Coach Rassas was a drill sergeant in his former life.

Promptly the next morning at 5:30 am, Coach Rassas was knocking on each dorm room while ringing a captain's bell in his other hand.

"It is a great day to be alive, so let's get started," Coach Rassas said with an authentic exuberance for life.

After a light breakfast, the attendees were directed outside.

"This is not about hiking until you drop," Coach Rassas said with a wry grin. "We want you to be in touch with nature. It is good for the soul."

For Trey, the 55-degree temperature was refreshing. Moreover, Coach Rassas's gung-ho spirit was contagious.

Trey did not look back. He went to the front of the line, in lockstep with Coach Rassas' double-time pace.

Trey had learned as a varsity letterman in high school track that he could set his pace if in the front of the line. If he were in the middle of the pack, the pace is disjointed with stopping and starting by using precious energy and more oxygen from a burgeoning heartbeat.

In the first leg of the hike, all attendees were directed to make a beeline to a small township—Conneaut—and ascend a hill overlooking a picturesque view of the Great Lake Erie.

There was stillness in the air as the fog was lifting over the calm waters. The air was tranquil, except for a fog horn intermittently sounding every 12 seconds from a nearby lighthouse.

As Trey and the other men were enjoying the moment, Coach Rassas blew a whistle, alerting the group to resume the hike.

But Mitch, who could transform from melancholy to vociferous indignation as quickly as a chameleon changes colors, had utter disdain for vociferous cacophonic noises.

Even when Mitch was seemingly congenial, he possessed a hard, judgmental eye, wary of depending on anyone.

He appeared almost spellbound in viewing the ambiance of the lake. He seemed to be in a non-agitated state, which was a rarity for him.

Among other things, Mitch had been diagnosed with misophonia and sensory processing disorders, which had been documented in his medical records that were forwarded to Dr. Snyder, Gerald, and Fr. Liam.

But that information had not been conveyed to Coach Rassas. In the immediate moments after the whistle was heard by anyone within a quarter mile, Mitchell could not contain himself.

Mitch's Damascus moment had arrived. He confronted Coach Rassas in a menacing-temerity manner.

Mitch was working himself into a frenzy. His face was beat red and his Adam's apple vexed while his temples pulsated.

Coach Rassas was bewildered but maintained a calmness, careful not to escalate Mitch's volatility.

But in the next few moments, Mitch's rage heightened.

"What the hell is your problem, coach?" Mitch said in an accusatory tone. "You could not allow us to feel good for two seconds.

"You tell us that this exercise is an opportunity for us to be in touch with nature," Mitch continued. "That is exactly what we were doing until you sadistically blow that whistle for us to continue on some kind of death march."

Fr. Liam and Gerald positioned their bodies between Coach Rassas and Mitch.

After a pause that seemed like an eternity under the circumstances, Gerald asked everyone to take a deep breath and decompress. Mitch reluctantly followed Gerald's lead.

But Mitch still was angry as he glared at Coach Rassas with a look that could kill.

At issue was whether Mitch was delusional, but no one disagreed that his perception that Coach Rassas was leading a death march was his reality.

Mitch accepted a bottle of spring water from Fr. Liam. After taking a few gulps, Mitch was asked by Dr. Synder to look at the birds near the shoreline.

As Mitch redirected his focus to the lake, his anger was placated. Dr. Synder then rendered an executive decision by interjecting, "Let's take this time to self-meditate and head back to the lodge for lunch."

Later that day, Dr. Synder, on behalf of the Wildness Program, apologized to Coach Rassass for not sharing Mitch's condition of misophonia. Dr. Synder told Coach Rassas and the entire staff they would be privy to essential medical issues of each attendee on an at-need basis.

Mitch's outburst had triggered a eureka moment for Trey, who had assumed the Wilderness Program was intended for him and other victims of bullying, hazing, and intimidation.

Trey wondered whether Mitchell and other attendees might be less like him and more like Randy.

Trey pondered whether he was in an asylum euphemistically dubbed a Wilderness Program.

Later that day, Trey approached Fr. Liam, who did not mince words when asked a direct question about the Wilderness Program.

Fr. Liam said the Wilderness Program is providing specific mental health treatments for each patient.

"Some of them have been bullied and others have been bullies," Fr. Liam bluntly told Trey. "Yet others are neither bullies nor victims, but diagnosed with documented afflictions.

"The bottom line," continued Fr. Liam, "is the Wilderness Program offers a variety of treatments for a diverse clientele."

The two men embraced before Fr. Liam added, "Please remember Trey that your challenges do not stem from a dysfunctional family. Your parents and siblings love you. Your mother held and read to you when you were an infant. You were not thrust into daycare as a mere toddler. You developed empathy and a well-formed conscience."

Fr. Liam contrasted Trey's upbringing with other patients who were raised in familial dysfunction.

"It does not excuse them for their behavior, but there are reasons why they are anti-social," Fr. Liam said.

Trey nodded as if he understood Fr. Liam's paradox. The two men briefly embraced before Fr. Liam winked while adding, "No hard feelings, Trey?"

Trey, straight-faced, responded, "I just have one question."

The wrinkles on Fr. Liam's face vexed as if he were perplexed, then invited the question by rotating his arms in a circular motion.

"What is on the menu for dinner and what time are we expected at the dining hall," Trey asked while his face morphed into a smile.

Both men effusively laughed as they parted company.

The next morning Trey arrived early for his first session with Gerald, who appeared non-threatening, slouched on a couch with droopy shoulders, and a gaunt face with sunken brown eyes.

Gerald's detached disposition belied his internal fire to mend those who were broken from no fault of their own. And, he was an acute listener.

Gerald, talking in a monotone, politely asked Trey to sit on a nearby couch.

Awaiting questions from Gerald, Trey was in a silent pensive mediated state. Aside from the steady ticking of a Grandfather's clock perched on a nearby armoire, he was lost in time, literally and figuratively.

In what seemed like a few seconds of relapse, Trey was in a state of prolonged neuralgia in which memories from his frontal lobe of conscious thought recessed in his subconscious.

This is exactly what Gerald had hoped would occur in preparation for the therapy session.

Gerald permitted Fr. Liam to join the sessions as an observer to provide solace for Trey. Gerald realized Fr. Liam might help discuss how Trey inculcated his Catholic faith to mercifully respond to bullies.

Gerald did not want to undermine Trey's faith but wanted to provide him with tools to effectively survive in a society rife with aggression.

Gerald was intrigued by the one notable exception in which Trey retaliated against his former high school antagonist, Randy. Gerald postulated that Trey's aggression against Randy was chemically induced.

Gerald wanted to test his theory by reenacting the incident with Randy to determine whether Trey's cerebral concentrates of serotonin would be lowered to induce anger ranging from passive-aggressive behavior to outright hostility.

Gerald's theory was based on a recent study of teenage boys prone to violence in which they reported low levels of serotonin led to proactive and reactive aggressiveness.

Gerald's objective was to prescribe cyproheptadine to prevent Trey's serotonin levels from rising. Then, Trey would be subjected to a hostile environment that triggers low levels of serotonin to induce an aggressive response.

Gerald believed this would provide Trey with appropriate aggression to stand his ground on an at-need basis. However, identifying the appropriate level of serotonin for Trey was not an easy task. If serotonin levels were lowered too much, Trey may be initiating overt aggression. Serotonin levels lowered insufficiently would not allow Trey to appropriately respond with aggression.

This process of how anger fuels behavior was experimental but had been discussed in psychology journals and even garnered national attention in a simplified manner when the American cinematic comedy—"Water Boy"—premiered several years ago. In the movie, the central figure—Bobby Boucher—became a star college football linebacker by visualizing those who had bullied him. That vision would engender anger, which he used as his tackling fuel to raise havoc against opposing quarterbacks.

Well before the movie premiered, Gerald was enamored with the concept that anger is essential as a line of defense to combat hostility. He was convinced the key is managing anger through chemical blockers to keep serotonin at a determined level.

Gerald had little doubt that for Trey to have any semblance of normalcy, he needed a level of anger to assert himself appropriately when interacting with aggressors.

Gerald knew this was anything but an exact science, but he was willing to proceed, albeit cautiously.

For good measure, Trey was injected with dopamine as a neurotransmitter to combat severe mood swings and depression.

Gerald peppered several questions for Trey, periodically invoking Randy's and Bryce's names to determine whether his demeanor changed. Initially, Trey remained placid.

But when Gerald mentioned Randy and Bryce in association with public shaming, Trey exhibited agitation by clenching his fists and clicking his heels.

Gerald continued to invoke Randy's name as Trey responded in the same manner.

Gerald, appearing to be breaking new ground, decided to follow up with a risky proposition by contacting the judge who had sentenced Randy to a 10-year probationary term for pleading no contest to two counts of assault.

Randy's probation precluded him from traveling outside of Florida.

Gerald asked through the Wilderness Program's legal counsel to petition a Pinellas County Circuit Judge for Randy's probation to be modified for him to travel to Ohio.

Judge Stephanie Blahut agreed to preside over a hearing on the issue. Randy expressed willingness to attend the Wilderness Program in the hope that it might bode for a reduction in his probationary term.

Gerald asked Fr. Liam to contact Trey's parents, who were considering litigation against Randy for compensatory and punitive damages stemming from Trey's mental anguish, torment, and suffering.

Fr. Liam advised Thomas and Katharine that a suit would impede Randy's willingness to participate in Trey's therapy sessions.

The Barrys agreed to drop the suit on two conditions: Gerald undersigned a sworn statement that Randy's participation in Trey's therapy is beneficial, and Randy cooperated fully with Gerald's directives.

The terms were agreed upon.

Judge Blahut, a former prosecutor reputed for sentencing criminal defendants on the high end of Florida's sentencing guidelines, granted the motion for Randy to travel to Conneaut for the express purpose to participate in Trey's therapy under Gerald's supervision.

Michael York, Randy's attorney, asked the judge to reduce Randy's probation.

Judge Blahut tersely responded, "Mr. York, you should know better than to ask me that question. You can file a motion to reduce probation on behalf of your client and I will take it under advisement."

Bryce, free and clear of any legal penalties, agreed to also participate in Trey's sessions.

Before Randy and Bryce were introduced in Trey's therapy sessions, Gerald wanted to obtain data from a Rorschach test, a psychological assessment in which Trey's perceptions from inkblots would be recorded to detect underlying thought processes that he had been reluctant to disclose.

As Trey became more comfortable with Gerald's self-effacing non-threatening manner, his feelings and incidents that had been repressed were elicited through weeks of sessions.

Gerald had been prepared for bullying incidents in Trey's childhood, but was aghast, even for a seasoned psychologist, to hear how Randy, Shelly, Bryce, Stephen, and Julie had destroyed him for their sheer amusement.

Gerald was on the cusp of forcing Trey into a deja vu situation in which a very risky experimental treatment could be a great victory or a colossal defeat. If the latter were to occur, Trey might never recover and his opportunity for a normal life would be vanquished.

Gerald was willing to roll the dice.

Chapter 11

De Ja Vu

As far as anyone knew, Randy was the only one on the planet to have incurred Trey's anger. Gerald was convinced Trey still had antipathy for Randy.

But what Gerald did not know was whether Trey's anger would be induced by future interactions with Randy. Moreover, would Randy's behavior be sufficiently repugnant for Trey's anger to be manifested?

Trey arrived early for his therapy session. He looked downward, feeling unflappable as if he did not have a worry.

Unbeknownst to Trey, Gerald nodded at Randy, who was seated at a corner table across the room. Right on cue, Randy stated in a clear, assertive voice, "Good morning Trey."

Trey instantly recoiled at hearing Randy's voice. How could he not? The incident with Randy was seared in Trey's mind for the balance of his natural life. The hair on the back of Trey's neck stood up.

Randy's voice instantly changed the vibe in the room. Randy was Trey's worst nightmare. As far as Trey was concerned, Randy was persona non grata at the Wildness Program and in his life, period.

For Trey, an invitation for the perfidious Randy to come face to face with him was an utter act of betrayal and utter callousness.

The mere presence of Randy had Trey combusting in full froth. His adrenaline was in overdrive. And, his fervor-pitched hostility indicated Trey's serotonin levels were decreasing.

Trey was morphing into someone other than himself in what seemed like warp speed for all to see. He turned toward Gerald with a menacing stare.

But Gerald remained unflinching, allowing the odious Randy to dutifully follow his script.

Randy annunciated in his best stentorian voice, "Where are your manners, Trey? I bid good morning to you."

Randy was comfortable in this role, flashing a faint smile.

At this moment, Trey was a bundle of nerves. He did not know what to say, if anything, to his nemesis.

Randy added, "What is the matter, Trey? Does the cat have your tongue?"

The antagonistic Randy intentionally paused as the silence in the room felt awkwardly protracted.

Randy sneered, reveling with hedonistic delight in his latest rendition to torment Trey. Randy then walked a few short steps, audaciously invading Trey's personal space.

Unmistakably, Randy was Trey's anathema.

In Trey's mind, Randy's only justification to re-appear in his life would be a mea culpa.

But Randy was anything but remorseful. His actions belied any sense of appropriate boundaries.

It was more than Trey could bear. His face was flush as drops of perspiration dripped from his brow. His hands were balled into fists.

There was every indication Trey was on the verge of implosion. He remained outwardly caustic as an inferno burned within.

When Randy placed his hand on Trey's chest, there was no turning back. At that moment, Randy did not fully realize he had once again lit the match for Trey's incendiary outburst.

Trey stepped backward, distancing himself from Randy. His voice quivered and then stated in amplification, "Touch me again and it will be the last time you ever do. Do you understand what I am saying to you, son of a bitch?"

Raw emotion was fueling Trey into overdrive.

Randy immediately turned his head and looked in Gerald's direction.

Gerald responded with a sardonic grin, realizing Trey's cathartic vitriol was sparked by his anger for Randy, thereby precipitously reducing his serotonin levels.

But Randy was concerned Trey was capable of anything. Randy wondered if Trey was carrying. No weapons were permitted for guests at the Wilderness Program.

Gerald, knowing Trey did not have a firearm, was willing to allow the diatribe to play out. He discreetly nodded for Randy to proceed.

But Randy stepped closer to Trey, who in one instantaneous swoop, pushed his hands into Randy's chest. Randy was propelled backward, stumbling and falling on his backside. Trey stepped over Randy and looked over him with his fists clenched, then added:

"'Do you want a piece of me, jackass?"

At that point, Gerald had seen enough, realizing there was more risk than reward to continue acrimonious exchanges.

Gerald asked Randy to exit the room, which he promptly did.

Following the session, Gerald asked Fr. Liam to find out whether Trey had any residual effects from the session.

Fr. Liam gave Trey time to decompress from the session, then approached his room. He heard an animated discussion in which Trey was engaged in emphatic soliloquies:

"I need to get the hell out of this God-forsaken place."

He felt a deep sense of betrayal from Gerald and Fr. Liam. And in his mind, the Wilderness Program was his condemned purgatory for attempting suicide.

As Fr. Liam continued to eavesdrop, Trey's comments were difficult for him to absorb:

"I pray for Mom and Dad to purge me from this hellhole. I have no friends here. Gerald is a Judas and Fr. Liam is joined at the hip with him. I will do what I have to do to not stay here for one more day."

Fr. Liam knew it would be an exercise in futility to talk with Trey in his state of mind. He then changed course, promptly texting Thomas:

"Everything we are doing is in Trey's best interest. Please be strong for him. Releasing him would be an irreversible error in judgment. Trust me."

Within moments, Thomas responded to the text. "We do trust you, Liam, but we need to know what is happening."

Fr. Liam expeditiously contacted Thomas via cell phone to bring him up to speed.

Thomas immediately picked up the call and pressed the speaker button on his phone for Katherine to hear Liam's every word.

Fr. Liam mostly talked in generalities, intimating there had been a few bumps in the road.

But Thomas vociferously interjected, "Talk to us, Liam. What in the hell does a few bumps in the road mean?"

Liam paused, then exhaled before responding:

"The interactions between Trey and Randy were intense, but were a breakthrough. We are on the right track.

"We can determine what Trey needs to visualize from his past for him to induce an appropriate level of anger for him to effectively fend for himself against aggression," Fr. Liam said.

Thomas and Katharine wanted Fr. Liam to expound upon "intense interaction."

But Fr. Liam did not want to delve into additional detail over the phone.

"It would be preferable for this conversation to be in-person," Fr. Liam advised.

Fr. Liam did not realize at this moment Thomas and Katharine had decided to board the next flight to Youngstown.

"We will be arriving at this Wilderness Program this evening," Thomas anxiously said.

As the phone call ended, Fr. Liam immediately circled the wagons by apprising Gerald and Dr. Synder of the Barrys' impending arrival.

There was agitation in Dr. Synder's voice as he directed Fr. Liam and Gerald to immediately meet with him.

Gerald and Fr. Liam briskly walked into the office of Dr. Synder, who was stone-faced, loosening his tie and shifting in his chair. He was not attempting to project anger in some sort of faux indignation but was eliciting raw emotion that comes from fear and insecurity.

Dr. Synder, without preamble, excoriated Gerald in a non-stop rant.

"You are not going to pin this on me, Gerald," Dr. Synder said, ignoring the fact that Gerald was not declaring Dr. Synder reprehensible. "You are the one willing to test boundaries to the detriment of your patients."

Dr. Synder gave credence to the gossip about Gerald as an enigmatic, quirky charlatan. Gerald, sitting in a chair across Dr. Synder's desk, involuntarily smirked, reflective of a nervous tic in his state of embarrassment.

But the smirk was perceived by Dr. Synder as ill-timed cockiness and arrogance, further infuriating him as his voice escalated into righteous fury.

Dr. Synder was unwilling to give Gerald the benefit of the doubt. Gerald realized his future was at stake based on Dr. Synder's edict.

Dr. Synder proceeded to lean over his desk and sigh unabashedly. The sigh was anything but involuntary. It was an intentional display of Dr. Synder's contempt for Gerald.

Dr. Synder then pointed his index finger at Gerald, gesturing for him to move closer.

As Gerald did so, Dr. Synder enunciated in a whisper:

"Do not make the mistake that I will turn a blind eye and deaf ear to this. Do I have your full attention, Dr. Faith?"

Gerald cleared his throat, then responded, "Absolutely Dr. Synder. You always have my full attention."

Gerald calmly disavowed himself as some type of junk-science charlatan engaged In dereliction of duty. He emphasized his work in ground-breaking clinical trials for patients such as Trey to have the tools to fend off aggression.

Gerald appeared poised, except for him occasionally pulling on his ear lobes. Inwardly, he was a bundle of nerves. However, if he were to emerge unscathed from this debacle, he would have to remain cool and collected.

To complicate matters, Gerald did not know how to repudiate harsh rebuke. He was a master of interpreting human behavior but was out of his comfort level when on the hot seat for castigation.

Dr. Synder then removed his glasses, reached for his handkerchief, and wiped the lenses as if it were the most pertinent task at that moment.

Dr. Synder wanted to bide time for Gerald to squirm. And then Dr. Synder capitulated:

"Now, let's move on to discuss our meeting with the Barrys."

Time was of the essence. It was half past 3 pm. The Barrys had sent a text message to Dr. Snyder indicating they would be at the Youngstown Airport by 4:30 pm and arriving at the Wilderness Program by early evening.

Dr. Synder asked the million-dollar question: "Is Trey making progress or is he retrograding?"

Gerald paused for effect as if he had to ponder the question. In reality, he had asked himself the very same question a hundred times over. Gerald said the short answer is "yes," but for Trey's treatment to come to fruition, he has to endure tense interactions with Randy and Bryce.

Gerald's blunt comment pleased Dr. Synder, who was prepared for him to engage in psycho-babble.

But Dr. Synder was not convinced the rewards outweigh the risks in Trey's treatment.

Gerald tactfully and assertively responded, "Trust can be restored over time, but there is no question that the potential for living a healthy life is worth the risk.

"Without the risk, there likely is no life worth living and possibly no life at all," Gerald said in a somewhat omniscient tone.

Dr. Synder, sitting on the edge of his chair, nodded as he faintly smiled.

Gerald intuitively knew at this moment Dr. Synder would be in his corner moving forward.

There was a long pause before Dr. Synder advised:

"If you keep it simple and speak from the heart, we will get through this, Gerald."

Gerald softly responded, "I understand." He then excused himself to collect his thoughts.

As Gerald was walking on the premises, he saw a car entering the parking lot. A man was behind the wheel and a woman was seated in the front passenger seat.

Gerald overcame his introverted proclivities and social awkwardness to greet the Barrys.

But Thomas and Katharine were distant. Thomas was borderline irascible. Gerald instantly realized their emotions vacillated between sadness, frustration, and a sense of betrayal.

Gerald did not apologize but expressed empathy for what they were enduring.

Gerald's outreach to the Barrys had little impact on their dispositions.

Thomas demanded that Trey be immediately released from the Wilderness Program.

Gerald realized if the Barrys saw their son at this time, Trey would be going home with them. Without hesitation, Gerald responded, "Trey is not available at the moment. Let me escort you to Dr. Synder's Office where we can answer all of your questions."

As they walked, Gerald subtly sent a text to Fr. Liam, asking him to meet the Barrys in Dr. Synder's office ASAP.

Once the Barrys, Dr. Synder, Gerald, and Fr. Liam gathered for a closed-door meeting, Thomas cut to the chase, demanding he and Katharine visit Trey immediately.

Dr. Synder politely deflected Thomas' request, suggesting Gerald provide the Barrys with a status report of Trey's therapy sessions.

But Thomas persisted: "We have a right to see our son."

Katharine chimed in too. "Nobody loves a child like a parent. Trey needs us and we need him."

Fr. Liam turned to Katharine, whose eyes were welling up with tears. He gently embraced her and in his quiet voice, said: "I can't imagine how you feel, but please know you are never alone."

Fr. Liam inconspicuously looked away from Katharine, staring at the heavens, and then extended his hand to Thomas.

Thomas clutched Fr. Liam's hand as the two men engaged in a robust handshake.

Fr. Liam made eye contact with Thomas, then spoke:

"Each of us is seeking what is best for Trey. Thomas and Katharine, you have to trust us. Please listen to Gerald as he verbally walks through Trey's treatments."

Dr. Synder once again yielded to Gerald, but this time the Barrys did not object.

Gerald mustered the courage to make eye contact with Thomas and Katharine, then pivoted to his narrative:

"Mr. and Mrs. Barry, the reality is conventional treatment may allow Trey to feel better for a provisional time, but will not change his behaviors to effectively cope against aggression in the real world.

"I want," Gerald said before pausing to rephrase, "we want Trey to have as normal a life as possible. But Trey's fragility will not allow him to have the quality of life unless he can assert himself when needed," Gerald deftly said.

Thomas interjected, "You should have consulted with us about the perils of having Randy and Bryce confronting Trey."

Thomas' voice then trailed off, knowing that he and Katharine were aware of an impending confrontation and there were no guarantees how Trey would react.

Fr. Liam approached Thomas and placed his arm around his shoulder as a friendly gesture for unification

Fr. Liam continued, recollecting Judge Blahut modifying Randy's probation for him to travel to the Wilderness Program. Thomas and Katharine were reminded that they had to sign an affidavit they would not sue Randy in order for him to participate in Trey's therapies.

The Barrys acknowledged the obvious but contended they were not sufficiently prepared to understand the level of torment their son would have to endure.

Gerald was prepared for that comment. He pulled a consent form from his coat pocket. The form, signed by the Barrys, absolved the Wildness Program from liability involving therapy sessions.

Thomas' face turned beat red as Katharine choked back sobs.

"Regardless of the damn consent form, what about a phone call to us?" Thomas asked. "You promised to keep us in the loop."

Thomas exhaled as if he were releasing pent-up frustration from a heavy heart.

Dr. Synder intervened, suggesting a 10-minute respite to decompress.

As Fr. Liam led the Barrys to a nearby kitchen where he poured two cups of coffee for them, Dr. Synder asked Gerald to remain seated in the office.

Dr. Synder had an ace up his sleeve. One of his closest colleagues was Dr. Dave Davenport, who hosted a syndicated television program about familial dysfunction and mental health therapy.

Dr. Synder had been advised that the Barrys were frequent viewers of the program.

In the aftermath of the interaction between Trey and Randy, Dr. Synder contacted Dr. Dave, who perused Trey's case file and agreed to consult with the Barrys.

"Gerald, the Barrys are still equivocating. Would you be ok with us patching Dr. Dave into a conference call with the Barrys?" Dr. Synder tactfully asked.

It was not lost on Gerald that Dr. Synder was modifying his approach, asking for approval instead of condemnation.

For Gerald, this was a no-brainer. The Wilderness Program needed reinforcements and Dr. Davenport was the ringer who could make it happen.

"God may be smiling on the Wilderness Program today," Dr. Synder said. "Dave sent me a text within the hour indicating he is available if need be."

Within minutes, Fr. Liam returned, but without the Barrys. Fr. Liam's face was flushed as he explained that the Barrys are attempting to locate Trey and leave the premises with him.

"Are they still here?" Dr. Synder asked. Fr. Liam answered that their rental car is in the parking lot.

Dr. Synder summoned a security guard to prohibit the Barrys from accessing the car and directed Fr. Liam to meet Trey.

Fr. Liam also sent a text to Thomas and Katharine, indicating Dr. Davenport is waiting to speak with them.

The text instantly captured Thomas and Katharine's attention, prompting them to call Fr. Liam by phone.

Fr. Liam immediately answered the call.

"We have Dr. Dave Davenport on Zoom waiting to talk with each of you."

The Barrys looked at each other with astonishment before Thomas answered:

"Ok Liam, we are heading to Dr. Snyder's office."

Dr. Synder, Fr. Liam, Gerald, and the Barrys gathered around a computer screen in which Dr. Dave was on full display as he introduced himself in his southern drawl.

Katharine momentarily gushed, enthralled to be in Dr. Dave's presence. A few seconds later, she composed herself as any good mother, listening to another mental health expert discuss her son's psychological condition.

Dr. Dave said he had perused Trey's medical history, then asked Thomas and Katharine, "Do you know the definition of insanity?"

The question was rhetorical, intended as a harbinger for discussion.

But Thomas and Katharine were perplexed. They looked at each other, shrugging their shoulders before Katharine responded.

"We probably do not know the technical definition, but we know it when we see it."

Dr. Dave politely smiled, then pivoted, suggesting routine counseling and therapy are not the solution.

"Traditional treatments will not effectively give Trey the tools he needs to cope in this world," Dr. Dave said.

Dr. Dave extolled the decision for Trey to visualize prior shame, engendering anger to combat aggression.

"Mr. and Mrs. Barry, this treatment is best for Trey and I know you want the best for your son," Dr. Dave said in his folksy unpretentious style.

Dr. Dave's comments had completely disarmed the Barrys. Thomas and Katharine relented.

"If Dr. Dave says this is the best course of action for our son, then we will stay the course," Thomas said.

Dr. Dave asked to be apprised of Trey's therapies. Dr. Synder assured him he would personally provide periodic and timely updates.

The animosity that had been in the air was no longer present. Trey was not going anywhere.

Chapter 12

Perception or Reality

"I can't believe my parents left me here in this God-forsaken hell hole," Trey said with disdain as he pounded iron with his compatriot, Mitch.

The workout was intended to mitigate Trey's anger, but it had the opposite effect. Mitch was an agitator, constantly in Trey's ear about the Wildness Program being rotten to the core.

Mitch was incapable of articulating melancholy cynicism. His modus operandi was to obsess about what he perceived as unmitigated exploitation.

Such was the case when he responded to Coach Rassas on that fateful early morning hike.

But now Mitch was lashing out not only at Coach Rassas but Dr. Synder, Gerald, Fr. Liam, and the entire Wilderness Program for what he considered systematic manipulation of their patients.

At best, Mitch and Trey had an unrequited friendship. Trey allowed Mitch to be Mitch. It was a one-sided relationship. Trey, dutifully conciliatory, thoughtfully listened to Mitch's bombastic views about the world.

On rare occasions, Trey would challenge Mitch based on his extreme and aberrant commentary. In those instances, their rapport suffered because Mitch did not take kindly to constructive criticism. In Mitch's mind, it was his way or the highway!

Mitch had an antithetical attitude that teetered on obstreperous obstructionism.

But unmistakably, Trey and Mitch were new best friends because they deplored the Wilderness Program. Mitch resented the Wilderness Program for ambushing Trey with Randy's presence. And, Trey realized he had become a psychological experiment.

After observing Trey and Mitch feeding off each other's discontent, Fr. Liam informed Gerald Trey was manifesting repeated aggression and angry outbursts.

In a meeting with Gerald, Fr. Liam shared a recent encounter with Trey.

"I approached Trey in the weight room and asked him to join me for lunch," the cleric said. "Trey stared at me as if I had two heads and told me, 'Padre, no lunch while working out. No pain, no gain.'"

Fr. Liam continued: "The thing about it, Gerald, he was terse, detached, and dismissive. Not outright rude, mind you, but damn near close.

"It was almost as if I had to do a double take," Fr. Liam said. "Who is this person and what happened to the old Trey."

Gerald paused, then offered, "This is a positive development, provided there is balance. We will need to be vigilant to ensure Trey's aggression does not spiral out of control."

But Fr. Liam was worried Trey's newfound aggression was intensifying, even without interactions with Randy and Bryce.

What would have been considered extreme behavior for Trey was becoming commonplace. Trey was transforming—figuratively and emotionally. He was force-feeding himself no small quantity of Creatine.

In just six short weeks since his arrival at the Wilderness Program, he had amassed 18 pounds of body weight.

Most of the added weight was brawn as Trey compulsively lifted weights as if he were a Hulk Hogan wannabe. And, Trey no longer shrugged his shoulders with "ah shucks" idle chatter. He rarely spoke, but when he did it was direct with an edge.

In his sojourn at the Wilderness Program, Trey had morphed from pacifist to passive-aggressive, to outright recalcitrant.

Trey's stubbornness to authority particularly intensified when he and Mitch were in the weight room.

For Trey and Mitch, strength conditioning was their only refuge in which they could be themselves and share their innermost thoughts, even if they were laden with dark cynicism.

During one workout, Trey told Mitch, "As far as I am concerned, the Wilderness Program sucks."

Mitch spontaneously pounced on Trey's comment with a question, "You know what we should do?"

Before Trey could answer, Mitch added with absolute temerity, "Let's blow up this hell hole?"

Mitch, emotionally and psychologically, was on the brink of a precipice. Trey glared at Mitch, whose left eye involuntarily twitched, which stemmed from his cognitive dissonance and nervous tics.

In this state, Mitch had a proclivity to utter nonsensical dribble.

But Trey deflected the absurd and focused on the pragmatic, responding with a subtle approach. He did not want to incite Mitch's fragile psyche.

Trey was well aware of how Mitch could mercurially transform from placid to a high-pitched fervor in a nano-second when his pent-up anxieties and sensory deprivation were triggered.

Trey cautiously and gently placed his hand on Mitch's shoulder to manifest one friend talking to another to quell discussion of a diabolical plot to destroy the Wildness Program.

But Mitch instantly flinched and abruptly stepped backward as Trey's hand fell to his side. That reaction was helping Trey understand Mitch's erratic behavior could not easily be explained.

Trey understood that Mitch, unlike Randy, was not a bully. Mitch had a sense of justice and a strong will to act when he perceived others were aggrieved. However, Trey realized what Mitch perceived as aggrieved, others would view as reasonable or justifiable.

Trey was beginning to understand aggression was a complicated emotional behavior and disorder. Mitch was exhibit A in which his distortion of reality was not learned, but biological. He was on the high end of the pervasive spectrum with a neurological disorder.

Even at his warmest, Mitch possessed a hard judgmental eye, wary of depending on anyone.

But Mitch's mother, Karen Hatcher, a middle-aged woman with long blond hair pinned in a bun, was in denial. Mitch was diagnosed with Autism as a three-year-old after an incident with Karen in which he violently kicked her after she attempted to hug him.

Throughout Mitch's youth, he was involved in countless fisticuffs. The fights usually occurred when someone invaded Mitch's personal space, either intentionally or unintentionally. Then all Hell would break loose when Mitch responded as if he were backed into a corner and fought for his perceived survival.

In these instances, Karen blamed other children, teachers, and his diet.

Karen defended her son by calling him a gifted child who was intellectually temperamental. It may have been poetic justice that her first name, Karen, was inculcated in the slang dictionary of popular culture as a woman who acts entitled and expects privilege.

Suffice it to say, Karen's name befitted her.

Regardless of whether Mitch was a boy genius, Karen continued to minimize his disorders by enrolling him in Brain Gym as a preadolescent.

Although Brain Gym was intended to hone sensory, fine motor, and academic-related skills, it did little to address Mitch's penchants for violence.

All too often sensory deprivation was the trigger for Mitch to implode. Brain Gym, however, confirmed Mitch deplored being touched due to his sensory deprivation.

Most of Mitch's behavioral challenges occurred in school. Teachers were unable to control Mitch's anger and unruly behavior. Mitch's classroom teachers at Pine View Middle School, a charter school within an upper-crust area of Williamsport, Pennsylvania exhorted Karen to have him medicated under the care of a physician or psychiatrist.

The teachers did not have licensed authority to prescribe medications for students but believed their classes would continue to be disrupted by Mitch unless his volatility and elopement issues were addressed by psychotropic drugs.

Karen reluctantly had Mitch evaluated by two behavioral therapists and a psychiatrist after she was informed that seclusion and restraint measures would be instituted unless his behavior was mitigated.

Under federal law, students with disabilities are to be educated in the least restrictive environment. However, states such as Pennsylvania have laws on the books to seclude and restrain students under extraordinary circumstances.

Dr. Ben Schapiro, a psychiatrist, prescribed low doses of a psychotropic drug, aripiprazole. Mitch's aggression and severe mood swings began to alleviate.

Over time, the drugs were less effective as Mitch's serotonin levels dropped, leading to aggression.

When Dr. Schapiro recommended higher dosages, Karen insisted all medications be discontinued. Predictably, Mitch's volatility was exacerbated, prompting three school suspensions before expulsion from Pine View.

Mitch was never secluded and restrained by the school. Karen contributed to politicians at the local, state, and federal level on both sides of the aisle to have access to public policy makers to get what she wanted.

In Karen's privileged life, rules, standards, policies, and laws did not apply to her. What mattered was calling-in favors for expediency.

Paradoxically, as Mitch's aggression continued through his teen years, Karen became increasingly in denial. Attempts to alter chemical imbalances in Mitch's brain had not been successful and as such, he was not placed on a waitlist for the Wildness Program.

For Karen, the fact the Wilderness Program was intended for pacifists such as Trey was an insignificant technicality.

Regardless of Mitch's afflictions, Karen wanted a powerful politician to intervene on her behalf for Mitch to be a priority applicant on the Wildness Program's waitlist.

Karen knew who to contact, U.S. Sen. Anthony Coppertelli, who promptly responded by threatening Dr. Synder and the Wilderness Program with federal funding cuts unless Mitch ascended to the top of the waitlist.

Dr. Synder relented and Mitch was welcomed into the Wilderness Program.

But Mitch was never a good fit in the Wilderness Program. And his behavior worsened, from the altercation with Coach Rassas to his contempt for the Program's leadership in the aftermath of Randy's participation in Trey's therapy session.

One evening before bed check, Trey and Mitch roamed the grounds at the Wilderness Program, embroiled in a tense conversation.

The conversation was punctuated with Mitch's declaration, "Trey, we have to make them pay for what they did to you. This is our mission in life. This is why we are here, to take down the Wilderness Program."

"Get that thought out of your head," Trey said. "You will do no such thing." Though Mitch did not argue with Trey at that moment, he did not acquiesce. He simply stared at Trey and then truculently disappeared in the still of the night.

In truth, this was quintessential Mitch. He always was looking for a crusade to vent against someone or something. He had found it with the alleged betrayal upon Trey.

Verbally gaslighting the Wildness Program was Mitch's fixation. And his internal fire from unabashed contempt for authority was fueling his declaration of war on the Wildness Program.

Mitch's world was akin to a Shakespearean tale. For every hero, there is a villain and for every force, there is an anti-force. Even when Mitch's life was seemingly at peace, he would have to invent conflict.

No one, not even Trey, realized Mitch's dissonance was teetering on a cataclysmic event at the Wildness Program. Mitch refused to acknowledge Dr. Synder, Gerald, and Fr. Liam were well-intentioned, wanting a better life for Trey.

But perception is reality and in Mitch's reality, Trey was entitled to vigilante justice. Mitch had convinced himself that his mission was to be Trey's defender for justice.

Trey did not share Mitch's sentiment and Mitch knew it. However, in Mitch's mind, this was a distinction without meaningful difference.

Regardless, Mitch would not allow anyone to impede his vindictive plan. His first order of business was to concoct an elaborate scheme for him to obtain materials to build a makeshift bomb.

He did so under the pretense of traveling to a nearby hardware store for supplies to make an ornate bird feeder.

Dr. Synder, Gerald, and Fr. Liam were duped into believing Mitch's assembly of a bird feeder was borne from sincerity.

Mitch was to follow protocols with a time-stamped departure and return to the Wildness Program, overseen by an intern, Ross McGregor.

Mitch operated surreptitiously, but announced the bombshell to Trey:

"The Wilderness Program will be no more."

Mitch wanted Trey to affirm him, suggesting he was inspired by a famous quote from President Teddy Roosevelt, also an American statesman, conservationist, historian, and writer.

Mitch told Trey, "It was almost as if President Roosevelt was talking to me when he said, 'Do what you can with what you have where you are.'"

But Trey grabbed Mitch by the shoulder and said, "President Roosevelt was talking about doing good, not creating domestic terrorism. Forget this nonsense, Mitch. This is crazy."

Mitch, with a bedeviled look in his eyes, responded, "Trey, it is too late. The bomb is to explode in two minutes in Dr. Synder's office."

Mitch had planted the device in a potted plant in Dr. Synder's office shortly before the Wilderness Program staff convened for their regularly scheduled noon meeting.

Trey sprinted as if he were in a 400-meter relay and screaming at the top of his lungs.

Dr. Synder, Gerald, and Fr. Liam heard Trey's screeching voice as they entered the front door of the office building. A moment later, a bomb exploded. The office was eviscerated as a conflagration erupted.

Each of them was inundated with falling debris. Blood was gushing from Dr. Synder's face. Emergency Medical Technicians responded within minutes, placing Dr. Synder on a stretcher and transporting him in an ambulance to a nearby hospital.

Fr. Liam and Gerald sustained scratches and bruises but were otherwise not seriously injured.

As Trey witnessed the devastation, he burst into tears as his mind was riddled with guilt.

"I could have prevented this," Trey said to no one in particular. "I should have taken Mitch's threats as seriously."

Gerald, overhearing Trey's comments, asked, "Did you know about this?"

Trey stuttered, trying to find his voice, then responded: "Mitch told me he wanted to blow up Dr. Synder's office, but I dismissed the comment as his typical hyperbole.

"I never thought he was capable of this," Trey said. "I should have known better."

At that moment, Fr. Liam, overhearing the conversation, approached Trey. Fr. Liam opened his arms, embracing Trey. The two men were locked together for several seconds.

Under his breath, Fr. Liam said, "You and I are brothers in Christ. The last few weeks have been a living hell for me, not knowing whether our friendship will be repaired."

As the two men unlocked their embrace, Trey said, "You are like family to me too. I am so sorry to have doubted you."

As Trey and Fr. Liam shook hands, Gerald interjected; "Is that Mitch?" Fr. Liam and Trey looked in the direction that Gerald gestured. Mitch was wide-eyed and mouth open. He then began to sprint on the road for vehicles departing from the Wilderness Program.

Gerald and Fr. Liam knew Mitch's appearance at the scene was like a pyro who watches the fire from relative proximity. Ashtabula police officers were already at the scene. Two patrol cars were in hot pursuit of Mitch, who had exited from a highway and was making a mad dash into the woodlands.

Police turned their K-9s loose. Within minutes, they found Mitch, holding a knife, threatening to slit his wrists. As officers moved in, Mitch attempted to slit the main vein in his left wrist. Officers restrained Mitch, allowing EMTs to impede bleeding and bandage the wound. Mitch was charged with three counts of attempted murder and one count of arson and detonating an explosive.

Chapter 13

The Verdict

Mitch contacted his mother from the Ashtabula County Jail. Karen wasted no time retaining a highly regarded criminal defense attorney, Timothy Derrickson.

He promptly had Mitch evaluated by mental health experts. The evaluations laid the groundwork for Attorney Derrickson to file motions asserting Mitch was incapable of providing adequate assistance in his defense due to mental instability.

Mitch angrily rebuked Attorney Derrickson, demanding Karen terminate him. In Mitch's mind, he knew right from wrong and was at odds with anyone who attempted to twist his righteousness into mental illness.

But this contentiousness became moot when Judge Patrick Donnelly denied Mr. Derrickson's motion. In his ruling, Judge Donnelly acknowledged Mitch's mercurial aggression, but determined his behavior did not prevent him from adequately aiding in his defense.

Several weeks later Mitch's trial commenced. There was a buzz as media photographers snapped images of Mitch, Karen, and Mr. Derrickson approaching the Ashtabula Courthouse.

Mr. Derrickson declined to comment, but Mitch proclaimed his innocence, adding Dr. Synder and the Wilderness Program should be on trial, not him.

That comment was the latest example that no one, including Attorney Derrickson, could control Mitch.

Once inside the courthouse, Mitch was seated quietly at the defense table, dressed in a navy blue suit with a traditional white shirt and beige tie. His long hair was parted in the middle and feathered back.

Casual observers would be forgiven if they mistakenly presumed Miitch as a well-put-together young man.

But those erudite in attire for defendants knew all too well that appearances are often deceptive. In his opening statement, Assistant State Attorney Hardy Prichard told jurors there is no dispute Mitch built the bomb that detonated, injuring Fr. Liam and Gerald and nearly killing Dr. Synder.

Prosecutor Pritchard said state witness Trey Barry will testify Mitch premeditated the attempted murder of the three victims because he wanted them to pay with their lives for what he perceived as cruel therapy strategies.

"Ladies and gentlemen of the jury, Trey will tell each of you his treatments forced him to revisit his nightmarish past. When Mitch found out about this, he plotted a violent vendetta against the Wildness Program despite Trey telling him vengeance is not an option."

And the jury, Prosecutor Prichard said, will hear from Psychiatrist Thomas Bane, who interviewed the defendant over several days and determined he met the legal test for the M'Naghten Rule – knowing the legality of right from wrong

But Attorney Derrickson countered Mitch's vengeance is associated with his protracted mental illness.

"By the time the defense rests its case," Mr. Derrickson said, "the jury will have heard from Psychiatrist Gary Hunter that Mitch suffered from an oppositional defiant disorder and believed he was protecting his friend, Trey, from further torment.

"There will be sufficient evidence Mitch is not guilty by reason of insanity," Mr. Derrickson said.

As Mr. Derrickson returned to the defense table, Mitch's eyes were transfixed on him.

Judge Donnelly also was watching Mitch, who pounded his right fist on the defense table. The judge asked the bailiff to escort the jury from the courtroom.

Judge Donnelly then asked Mitch if he understood trial decorum. Mitch initially shook his head, then proceeded to stand. Judge Donnelly ordered Mitch to sit. When he refused, the judge ordered the bailiff to secure the defendant.

Mitch began to escalate, screaming, "Do not touch me, you son of a bitch" as Bailiff Jack Beamer placed the defendant in handcuffs and ankle restraints.

Mitch was now in full mode of diatribe as he told the judge that his attorney is falsely portraying him as crazy.

"My attorney is a lying bastard," Mitch said. His outbursts drew the ire of Judge Donnelly, who immediately pounded his gavel.

In no uncertain words, the judge told the defendant such outbursts and breaches of court etiquette would not be tolerated.

"If there are any further outbursts from the defendant, he will be held in contempt of court and removed from the courtroom, " Judge Donnelly said with animus in his voice. Does the defendant understand?"

Mitch nodded and Mr. Derrickson answered "yes."

But no one, not even Mitch, knew whether he would conform to courtroom protocol. However, Mitch's proclivity for imploding made him an odds-on favorite to be held in contempt of court and removed from the courtroom before a verdict is delivered.

Judge Donnelly asked the attorneys whether there were any other issues to discuss before summoning the jury.

In light of Mitch's behavior, Attorney Derrickson then asked Judge Donnelly to reconsider his motion that the defendant is incapable of assisting in his defense.

Prosecutor Pritchard stood, buttoned his 48 large sport coat, and asked if he could be heard on the matter.

"Yes, but be brief," Judge Donnelly said in a firm-calm voice.

"Your honor, this is theater by the defense," Prosecutor Pritchard said. "The defense is orchestrating the groundwork to suggest the defendant did not receive a fair trial because he was unable to assist in his defense."

Judge Donnelly did not rule on the defense motion at this time. He peered at Attorney Derrickson through his wire-rimmed reading glasses, which were on the bridge of his nose, suggesting the defense motion may be reconsidered at a later point in the trial.

As the state presented its case, Mitch dutifully heeded Judge Donnelly's admonitions. Mitch took copious notes of the state's witnesses and even suggested inconsistencies in their testimony.

Mitch listened intently when Trey testified. Mitch did not take umbrage over Trey's testimony because their memories of past events aligned.

But during cross-examination, Mitch's face turned crimson as Attorney Derrickson grilled Trey.

"You knew Mitch was fiercely loyal to his friends and upset that you had to endure treatment in which you came face to face with someone who had once bullied you into submission" Attorney Derickson asserted in questioning Trey.

"In retrospect," Trey answered, "I should have done more. But at the time, I thought Mitch was simply blowing off steam."

Attorney Derrickson continued: "Would this incident have been avoided if you had perceived Mitch's threat as real?"

Trey, looking downward as he answered, "quite possibly."

As Trey exited from the witness stand, he looked at Mitch, who crossed his hands across his chest symbolizing his friendship with him. It was an odd moment as the defendant non-verbally communicated an enduring bond with the state's key witness.

But oddity appears to be the signature card of the egocentric Mitch. The following day, the state rested its case backed by Trey's testimony and expert witness Dr. Bane, who told jurors Mitch suffers from bipolar disorder and is on the pervasive spectrum for autism.

But Psychiatrist Bane said the defendant's aggression did not preclude him from understanding the crime of building a bomb with the intent to do great bodily harm to Dr. Synder and the Wildness Program Staff.

Dr. Bane conceded on cross-examination there is a possibility that Miitch's anger could have boiled into a vindictive compulsion that clouded his ability to discern right and wrong.

After the state rested its case, Judge Donnelly asked the defense to call its first witness. There was a gasp when Dr. Synder was called to the witness stand.

Dr. Synder, a thin man before the bombing, appeared frail, needing a walker to make his way to the witness stand.

Attorney Derrickson knew all too well Dr. Synder's testimony was a risky proposition. Jurors could empathize with Dr. Snyder and want Mitch to be held responsible for nearly killing him.

But the defense strategy was for the jury to perceive Mitch as a victim too. Under the defense theory of the case, the Wilderness Program's treatment of Trey triggered Mitch to implode and as such, these dynamics, in combination with Mitch's chemically imbalanced aggression, made him a ticking time bomb.

Attorney Derrickson wasted no time, asking whether the Wilderness Program is intended to treat aggression.

"No sir, " Dr. Synder answered. Attorney Derrickson quickly followed up, "Why was the defendant placed in the program?

Dr. Synder answered, "There were threats that our federal funds would be discontinued unless Mitch was enrolled."

"Who's made the threats?" asked Mr. Derrickson. "Sen. Coppertelli," answered Dr. Synder. Dr. Synder's testimony followed his deposition verbatim, telling jurors one of Sen. Coppertelli's wealthy constituents demanded that her son, reputed for violent outbursts, be placed in the Wilderness Program.

Dr. Synder then was asked whether the explosion would have occurred if the Wilderness Program was not leveraged to accept Mitch into the program.

Prosecutor Prichard objected, stating that the question calls for the witness to engage in speculation.

But Judge Donnelly permitted the question to be answered.

"Yes, I believe Mitch's enrollment in the program and the bombing go hand in hand," Dr. Synder said, "Mitch is the only patient to be placed in the Wilderness Program with acute aggression.

"Outside of Mitch, our patients are reticent, submissive individuals who need coping skills to survive against aggression."

The next defense witness, Dr. Hunter, testified Mitch suffers from severe mood swings and impulsive aggression.

In concluding his testimony, Dr. Hunter was asked whether Mitch met the legal standard to know right from wrong.

"Mitch's misguided but sincere allegiance to Trey was too much for him to manage mentally and emotionally," Dr. Hunter said. "These circumstances triggered anger and a vindictive spirit that clouded his ability to know right from wrong.

"In my opinion, Mitch's anger fueled a crusade to get justice for Trey, and in doing so, he did not have the mental acuity to appreciate the consequences of his actions."

Mitch mumbled under his breath, "Lies, all lies." In Mitch's mind, unadulterated lying is unforgivable and Dr. Hunter is a hired gun who is paid exceedingly well to lie.

But Dr. Hunter's testimony was compelling as each of the jurors listened intently. However, Prosecutor Pritchard may have created doubt in Dr. Hunter's testimony by noting on cross-examination that the expert witness had never concluded that any defendant met the legal standard of knowing right from wrong.

When the next witness was called to testify, Mitch's face appeared as if it were frozen momentarily and his back stiffened against the chair at the defense table. His eyes were transfixed on the witness, who was none other than his mother.

Karen walked with purpose to the witness stand and looked downward, careful not to make eye contact with her son. Karen was an attractive middle-aged woman. Her fashionable black-rimmed glasses complemented her professional-looking appearance. She, however, had never had a 9-5 job.

Karen inherited millions when her husband, Dieter, suddenly passed away five years ago from a massive heart attack. Her first order of business was to sell Dieter's governmental consulting group. She had no problem calling in favors from politicos, but otherwise had an aversion for them. She had observed her husband survive in the cutthroat world of big money and high-powered politics. Her disdain for politics was emboldened as she watched her husband waking up at dawn to communicate to a network of supporters and sucking up to power brokers with political posts on Facebook, Instagram, Twitter, and via email. His daily conquests were euphemisms for apologies, brown-nosing, and mind-mumbling humility in a cesspool known as his work environment.

Mitch was on edge, running his hands through neatly groomed hair as he ruminated nervously about what his mother was going to say about him.

As Karen testified, Mitch murmured, "Please don't, please don't, Mom." Mitch could not bear for his mother to perjure herself for him. Within moments, Mitch's worst fears were evident. In response to open-ended questions from Attorney Derrickson, Karen portrayed her son as mentally unstable.

As she looked away from her son, she said, "Mitch was not in touch with reality. He would misinterpret behavior from teachers, coaches, classmates, and neighbors as if they were evil and must pay for their transgressions.

"This is why Mitch lived in a fantasy world and his behavior was unpredictable," she told the court.

But this was more than Mitch could handle. As his eyes welled with tears, he stood and beseeched his mom.

"Why are you lying about me, Mom?" he asked.

At that moment, Judge Donnelly pounded his gavel, ordering Mitch to be seated. When Mitch did not immediately heed Judge Donnelly's directive, the jurist ordered the bailiff to remove Mitch from the courtroom.

Mitch was charged with contempt of court, but allowed to return to the courtroom for closing arguments.

In final arguments, Attorney Derrickson summarized Karen's testimony:

"The Wildness Program was not equipped to treat those such as Mitch who are violent, delusional, and suffer from oppositional disorder behavior. Karen was desperate for her son to be treated and the Wildness Program symbolized in her mind one last gasp of hope for him to make a complete recovery.

"No one loves Mitch more than his mother," he said. "She was trying to do right for her son. But through no fault of his own, Mitch was placed in the Wilderness Program and predictably responded like the mentally imbalanced person he is when Trey Barry became distraught after undergoing questionable treatments."

But Prosecutor Pritchard responded that other than Karen and Dr. Hunter, no other witnesses described Mitch as not knowing the legal standard of right from wrong.

"Where are the teachers, coaches, and neighbors whom Mitch supposedly attacked?" asked the prosecutor.

As the jury deliberated, Attorney Derrickson knew all too well that juries seldom reach a not-guilty verdict by reason of insanity.

But three and a half hours later, the jury returned a verdict: Not guilty by reason of insanity.

In many respects, the verdict was a nightmare for the Wilderness Program, setting off a firestorm of questions:

Why Mitch was allowed to matriculate in the Wildness Program; Why Mitch was allowed to remain in the program even when he violently confronted Coach Rassas; Why Trey was subjected to questionable treatment; Why Mitch was permitted to freely purchase items from a local hardware store to build a bomb.

The verdict was merely the beginning to probe for answers and determine who is responsible for the aforementioned series of dubious decisions.

The verdict in the criminal case laid the groundwork for possible civil litigation against Sen. Coppertelli, Karen, and the Wildness Program.

There was one certainty as the fuzzy picture came into focus: There would be hell to pay.

Thirty days later there was a hearing to determine Mitch's future.

Attorney Derrickson asked for Mitch to receive an absolute discharge, arguing he no longer is a threat to others.

But Judge Donnelly imposed a supervision order for Mitch to remain at the Youngstown Mental Health Center Hospital. He ordered the hospital to follow up with a report within six months to revisit Mitch's mental health status.

Chapter 14

Trey on the Prowl

Trey had read the daily news articles about Mitch's trial. Following the verdict, he contacted Mitch via cell phone with congratulations. They exchanged pleasantries and called one another friends for life.

"Don't let the bastards get you down," Trey said in his parting comment to Mitch.

Trey's comment was noteworthy. It was as if he were telling Mitch not to endure B.S. from anyone.

Trey was not a finished product. His therapy sessions were suspended following the explosion in Dr. Synder's office. No longer was Trey the consummate pacifist who turned the other cheek at the first hint of aggression. His pent-up hostilities were uncorked and bubbling over.

Trey's confrontation with Randy and the strategies for him to visualize hostility to lower serotonin levels had altered his emotions to make him to be a more frequent aggressor. But Trey's beat downs had taught him lessons that ignoring bullies in a false reality empowers them.

No longer did he live life by the informal definition of insanity: repeating the same actions and expecting a different result. For the first time in Trey's life, he was claiming his independence, having a one-bedroom apartment in the enclave of Gulfport, which was a skip and a hop from the Suncoast beaches.

Thomas and Katharine would have preferred Trey to live with them. They wanted to keep watchful eyes on their fragile son.

But Trey was 22, having experienced enough torment for a lifetime. He wanted to live alone and there was not much, if anything, his parents could do about that.

Like many young people, Trey was learning independence comes with a morass of daily challenges—paying rent, utilities, groceries, vehicle maintenance, and so many other ancillary obligations.

Solace for Thomas and Katharine was knowing Trey resided a mere five miles from them. They did not want to be helicopter parents, but Katharine would deliver impromptu meals, and Thomas periodically brought a cooler of water bottles and a few beers, along with a DVD, for father and son bonding.

Trey traded in his Volkswagen Beattie for an older model Ford 150 pickup truck, which was bare bones except for an AM/FM radio and air conditioning, essential to withstand the torrid heat in the Sunshine State.

Trey supported himself by working two part-time jobs: clerk in the bait and tackle shop at O'Neill's Marina. His day began early, tending to the fuel dock and selling live bait and other supplies to fishermen before sunrise.

Trey transitioned late morning to a fiberglass repair shop. These jobs did not ensconce him in wealth, but they allowed him to support himself in relatively low-stress work.

Trey's family was his first love, but boating was his passion. Although boating and beach life tended to create a laid-back lifestyle, he was anything but a chilled dude.

The new version of Trey fixated on a crusade to reinvent himself with a vindictive spirit by intentionally recollecting past hostilities, fueling his aggression.

When in therapy, the lowering of the serotonin levels was more of an exception than the norm. But in recent weeks, Trey had become compulsive about calling to mind memories that would lower these levels. And, the sequence of flashbacks and the lowering of levels not only were occurring with greater frequency but with relative ease.

Trey's aggression was becoming more of the norm than the exception. He was ripped more than ever as his appetite to pound iron was as insatiable as ever.

Moreover, he was enrolled in a Korean martial arts class of taekwondo. He was fastidious in the techniques of martial arts, readily honing head-height kicks and jumping and spinning maneuvers.

Trey was anxious to apply these skills in the real world by confronting bullies on the streets.

For the first time in Trey's life, he was in attack mode to come to the aid of those who were easy marks. He wanted to be at the beckon call for victims in a way no one had been there for him.

But he also was going back to the future. By engaging in fisticuffs, he not only was fighting for future victims but also making up for years when he did not fight back.

Trey was well aware that in every generation since the American Revolutionary War, victimization also applied to groups, such as new immigrants looking for a better way of life in the United States.

As an Irish Catholic, he was well versed in Irish Need Not Apply (INNA) for jobs as first-generation Americans. Moreover, Thomas had told young Trey about the KKK burning crosses at homes of Catholic families.

But the darkest blights on American society were slavery and the genocide of Native Americans, followed by Japanese Americans placed in concentration camps during WWII.

Trey realized there were more recent examples of hate groups targeting minorities in Charlottesville, Virginia, gays in an Orlando nightclub, bombings in synagogues and vandalizing Catholic Churches, and targeting Catholic school students who were verbally crucified on cable news and social media for participating in a pro-life march in Washington DC.

The Washington Post, CNN, and celebrities rushed to judgment, opining that videos of the event depicted the students as disrespectful toward a Native American.

But the full unadulterated video elucidated that the students were singing the school's fight song in response to racial, bigoted, and vulgar taunts from other groups. A student who was accused of disrespecting a Native American was simply idly standing close to him.

After the Pro-Life Rally, the Catholic school where the students attended was forced to temporarily close due to death threats. The parents of one of the students sued the Post for defamation of character. Trey pondered whether the students would have been protected from public condemnation if they had been a different religion or no religion and had not been pro-life.

The answer to that question called for speculation, but what was abundantly clear is respect and dignity are arbitrarily applied to select Americans.

Trey had no pretense he would change the world around him. The new Trey, however, was convinced he could make a difference one individual at a time by exploiting the evil ways of Randy, Bryce, and others like them.

His first order of business was to contact Detective Gronkowski about locating Bryce.

Bruce said no criminal charges were filed against Bryce, Stephen, and Julie for setting up Trey's humiliation in the Florida Legislature.

There was an awkward silence for a few moments until Bruce revealed that Bryce had been terminated from his position at the Florida Legislature and blackballed from lobbying firms in Florida.

"Bryce has toiled in relative obscurity," Bruce said.

Trey remained mum before responding:

"Come hell or high water, Bryce will receive justice for his transgressions."

In many respects, Trey was at a crossroads: Was he going to be better or bitter? It appeared, at least at this moment, the answer was the latter.

"A defamation suit requesting an unspecified amount of damages for mental anguish, including public shaming, is your best course of action to settle the score against Bryce," Bruce said.

But Trey did not want to hear Bruce's advice.

"There is no way I am going to sue an unemployed legislative aide," Trey said. "What I am asking is how to find Bryce."

Bruce, relented, empathizing with Trey.

Bruce sifted through his copious notes, then added Bryce is a creature of habit, attending a watering hole like clockwork.

"Per my surveillance of Bryce, he frequents Pen Rods Café on North Dale Mabry in Tampa. I would start there," Bruce said.

There was no turning back for Trey with this newfound information.

He wanted to be a brawler with a new approach to kick ass and take no prisoners and in doing so, to force those who had made his life a living hell to expiate for their evil ways.

Trey's mindset was to stand toe to toe with Bryce, giving him a taste of his own medicine.

Beyond that, Trey's hatred for Bryce was metastasizing. His adrenaline was at full froth as he had an ominous "eye of the tiger" look with his fists balled as he entered Pen Rod's Café the following Wednesday with a truculent mindset.

Within moments, Trey scanned the café and had Bryce in his vision.

Trey's strategy was to trash-talk Bryce until he threw the first punch. Trey had one rule in his new code of conduct: do not throw the first punch.

Bryce was imbibing on Crown Royal, his drink of choice. Bryce was convinced Crown Royal was the best whiskey money could buy and true to his socio-path mindset, he deserved the best because he was the best.

But Bryce was not on his game and he could not find his swagger as Trey was invading his personal space. Bryce's face became flush, his fingers numb. Bryce felt as if he were in a catatonic state and his drink slipped from his fingers, falling on the floor.

Trey, without hesitation, moved a step closer to Bryce, then said, "What is wrong, Bryce? You look like you just saw a ghost."

Bryce looked downward, careful not to make eye contact. Attempting to recover, Bryce asked, "Are you stalking me?"

Trey adroitly defected the question, asking Bryce who will be his next target.

"It is not like that, Trey," Bryce explained. "Like you. I suffer from psychological issues."

Trey was bewildered at Bryce's suggestion they were more alike than different.

Bryce to his credit, added, "Of course, we have mental issues for different reasons. "You have been victimized throughout your life; I have suffered from schizophrenia as a young child," he said.

Bryce paused, then continued: "The point is I am mentally flawed not by choice, but due to chemical imbalances in my body."

Trey had an empathetic moment for Bryce. However, Trey took umbrage for Brcye to portray himself as a victim.

"Your psychological disorders and chemical imbalances do not explain everything," Trey said. "You are a sociopath who drove me to attempt suicide."

Bruce softly uttered a mea culpa.

"What I did to you was unthinkable," Bryce said. "I am finally receiving therapy to be a better person."

This was Bryce's attempt at public penance – an initial step in recovery.

Bryce probably should have stopped there, but he continued: "You are judging me based on the darkest time of my life. "Not a single one of us, not even you, Trey, wants to be judged based on his or her worst behavior."

Trey acknowledged inwardly that Bryce had made a compelling point. At this moment, Trey remembered the parable in which a cadre of men was preparing to stone to death a philandering woman. The men asked Jesus what to do, assuming they had trapped him in an unenviable position.

But Jesus responded, "Let the man who has not sinned cast the first stone."

One by one, the men dropped their stones and left. Trey did not know whether Bryce was incapable of rehabilitation, but would not judge him henceforth.

"Bryce, you will have to earn my trust, but I wish you no malice," Trey said.

Trey contemplated whether a socio-path with the depravity of Bryce would be willing to place his needs secondary to God or anyone else.

Trey realized anything is possible through God, but he was not ready to embrace Bryce's self-professed conversion. Parroting the oft-repeated quote from Maya Angelou of Oprah Show fame, Trey responded, "When people show you who they are, believe them the first time."

Trey then added, "Bryce, you clearly showed your quintessential self as a social path. "Once a SOB, always a SOB," Trey said, his eyes preening as if he were looking through Bryce.

Trey was not giving Bryce what he wanted at this moment: leniency.

"I am here, Bryce" Trey said, "to ensure there are no other victims.

"I am going to be on you like a bloodhound looking for his next meal," Trey said, sounding like a good ole boy with an ax to grind.

As Trey began to part company, he stopped and bellowed Bryce's name. All eyes in the cafe were on Trey and Bryce. Suddenly, there was silence within the cafe.

Trey gestured at the manager of the cafe, then added, "Where this man (Bryce) goes, there is trouble. You would be well advised to stop him at the door."

One of the patrons who happened to be watching the drama was none other than Captain Garza, who followed Trey to the parking lot.

"Trey, Trey, slow down," Captain. Garza said as if he were barking orders to his crew. "Do you have time for an old friend?"

Trey continued toward his truck, ignoring the voice. As Trey entered his vehicle, he gazed at the man who was trailing him. Trey recognized Captain Garza and cursed his predicament under his breath. He was irascible and in no mood for a kumbaya moment with an old friend.

But he had a special place in his heart for Captain Garza, Jake, and Zack. They had rescued him from the Bay waters and visited him at the hospital.

Trey attempted to mask his confluence of emotions and put forth his best self. He feigned a smile and extended his hand to Captain. Garza.

The two men robustly shook hands as Captain Garza locked eyes on Trey.

Trey looked downward. He could not sustain eye contact because he was uncomfortable with Captain Garza having observed what had transpired with Bryce.

Captain Garza then patted Trey on the shoulder and smiled.

As Captain Garza began to speak, Trey interrupted. "Sorry, you had to see that."

Captain Garza, without missing a beat, responded, "I am not sorry. It is obvious you are no longer the man we rescued last March."

Trey was befuddled by Captain Garza's comment. Was the captain complimenting him for his newfound bravado, or criticizing him for his tempestuousness?

Trey deflected the comment, then Captain Garza added, "It looked like you had a beef with the man whom you confronted."

Trey, unmasking his foul mood, said "damn straight."

Captain. Garza was temporarily startled. He was pleased Trey was no longer the submissive punching bag who had been plucked out of the seawater several months earlier, but Trey's emphatic "damn straight" comment suggested he was hardened.

"I know you are not asking for advice, Trey, but can I share what I consider a tidbit of advice that has served me well?" Captain. Garza asked.

Trey shrugged his shoulders as if he were acquiescing. Captain Garza was not going to allow Trey's nonchalant response to preclude him from offering an aspirational nugget of wisdom.

"There is a line between defending yourself and accosting someone," Captain Garza said. "Self-defense is not taking the fight to someone. I am a man of faith," Captain. Garza said, laying a predicate.

"My parents, God rest their souls, were devout Catholics. They passed their belief in God to me and my brothers and sisters.

"What my faith has taught me is that the ends never justify the means," Captain. Garza continued.

"Young man, I tell you, how we treat each person in accordance with Gospel Values is more important than producing a salutary result," Captain Garza said.

The captain extended his right hand outwardly before embracing Trey in a bear hug while whispering, "I am so proud of you, Trey.

'You have the will to never again be subjected to a living hell," Captain Garza said.

As the two men relinquished their embrace and began to part company, Captain. Garza turned and called to Trey with a wink: "Remember, you can't change the wind, but you can adjust the sails."

The half grin on Captain Garza's face disappeared as he added: "Never, never be one of those SOB thugs. You are better than that."

Trey nodded, then climbed into his truck and did not look back.

Chapter 15

Primrose Path

Capt. Garza's comments had piqued Trey's interest. For days, Trey pondered Captain Garza's advice is to take the moral high road.

But Trey could not detach his pent-up feelings.

Trey was guilt-ridden for not fighting back against bullies. He was of the mindset that his public shaming could have been avoided or alleviated if he had fought back. Trey was in a state of intransigence. The ugly memories not only haunted him but scarred him with indelible bitterness and an abiding vindictive spirit.

The combination of these factors, with his more frequent low levels of serotonin, left him incapable of heeding Captain Garza's advice.

Trey continued to be a weekly visitor at Penrod Cafe in his vigilance to pursue Bryce. In addition, he contacted Bruce to find out if he could elicit the whereabouts of Randy, Julie, and Stephen.

In the interim, Trey trolled a dive bar in the red light district along Nebraska Avenue in Tampa to protect law-abiding citizens from drug dealers, thugs, and prostitutes. One evening he steered his truck into the parking lot of a prototypical-looking seedy bar known as the "Library Lounge."

Trey knew he was in the right place to come to the aid of potential crime victims.

As Trey entered the front door, he instantly felt the penetrating stares of seemingly regular patrons who were sizing him up. He briefly hesitated, careful not to make eye contact with anyone, before strutting with purpose to the bar.

An emaciated-looking middle-aged woman behind the bar caterwauled, "Hey boy, you do not look like you are from these parts."

Trey simply said, "I'll take whatever you have on tap."

The woman forced a slight smile, exposing two severely upper chipped teeth. After scooting a mug of beer along the counter, she stood with hands on her hips and said, "What is the matter, boy?"

Trey now had empathy for the barmaid, realizing her chipped teeth may be the result of domestic violence. Clutching the mug and taking a sip of beer, Trey wanted to blend in with the other patrons, but do so without alienating her.

"I was born and raised in the Tampa Bay Area, but this is my first time here," Trey said. The woman extended her hand. She and Trey shook hands before she added:

"Nice to meet you. My name is Cynthia, but everyone calls me Cyn. "That is Cyn as she annunciated C Y N, not S I N," she said, giggling.

Cyn knew all too well that men like Trey do not come into her life. The typical patron was likely a high school dropout turned small-time criminal who was a drug dealer, pimp, or gang banger. Regardless of their variances in criminal activity, they lived by the code to take from others; don't let others take from them.

Cyn's flirtatiousness with Trey did not sit well with her on-again, off-again boyfriend, who was nicknamed Mad Dog for his menacing physical appearance.

At 6 feet, four inches tall, and with a 250-pound body permeated with tattoos and piercings, Mad Dog had a crazed look with dark brown eyes as wide as saucers. He could be mistaken as a Neanderthal with thick, curly uncombed hair and a full dark beard. His appearance projected piratical nerve with a vaudevillian style that intimidated local thugs and small-time hoods.

For Mad Dog, any dalliance involving Cyn was unacceptable. He was hell-bent no other man was going to take his girlfriend from him. To exacerbate matters, Mad Dog was on the verge of inebriation. He had been drinking straight whisky for the past two hours.

Mad Dog ominously starred at Trey. It was his death look. Trey did not flinch. He locked eyes with Mad Dog, much like Rocky meeting Mr. T's glare in Rocky III.

But Mad Dog approached Cyn as if he were intending to accost her. In one seamless motion, he reached over the counter of the bar and clutched Cyn's T-shirt, forcing the neckline to drape down to her breasts. The mangled red T-shirt with a white-letter inscription—"Girls do not study at the library"—manifested that Cyn was braless. She attempted to reconfigure the T-shirt, but it was like a luffing sail dead in the wind.

Cyn, with a beer in hand, flung it at Mad Dog. If Mad Dog were not already incensed, he was now. As he reached over the counter, Cyn spun backward.

Trey could not idly sit back, but he knew intervening on behalf of Cyn could cost him his life or irreparable bodily harm. In the next fleeting second, Trey horse-collared Mad Dog, who appeared subdued.

Within moments, Trey lessened his grip on him. But Mad Dog was far from finished.

"What you start, I finish," Mad Dog said with a sneer-crazed look, conveniently forgetting he was the impetus for the altercation. Mad Dog wasted no time escalating the fracas. He picked up a chair and flung it at Trey's upper body. The chair was not Mad Dog's weapon of choice, but it was within his ready reach to use it as a missile.

The chair whisked by Trey's head, smacking against his right shoulder. Trey screeched from the immediate pain. Mad Dog momentarily paused, letting his guard down.

Trey, relying on his newfound taekwondo skills, ultimately extended his right leg to Mad Dog's chest, knocking him back with the tenacity of a middle linebacker. This did not sit well with other patrons, all of whom knew Mad Dog.

Trey was not just a stranger. He was quickly becoming enemy number one, at least within the confines of the Library Lounge. The vast majority of the patrons wanted Mad Dog to have an unfair advantage over Trey.

There was a frail-looking middle-aged man between Trey and the exit. Trey made a mad rush to the door, running over the smallish man. Trey ran for his truck like there was no tomorrow as the others gave chase.

Trey stumbled and nearly fell in the sandy-pebble-laden parking lot. He quickly recovered to see his truck directly ahead of him. With others in hot pursuit, Trey did not have time to reach into the front pocket of his jeans for the truck keys and click to unlock the driver's side door. As he lunged for the door handle on the truck, he realized the door was unlocked.

"Thank God," he said under his breath. In one seamless motion, Trey opened the door and jumped into the truck. He immediately locked the door. Seconds later the motley cadre of pursuers had descended on Trey's truck.

It was as if they were a pack of crazed dogs in a feeding frenzy. A tall-slender man with shoulder-length greasy-oiled hair catapulted on the hood of the truck and was pounding his fists on the windshield.

Another man, burley and bearded, ferociously tugged on the door handle as his eyes bulged with hedonistic delight. He was pursuing Trey like a crazed dog wanting red meat.

As Trey peripherally saw a man jabbing the truck's left front tire with a switch-blade knife, he placed the truck key in the ignition and turned it. The engine immediately turned over.

Trey shifted the truck forward and stomped on the gas pedal. The rear wheels momentarily spun, spitting pebbles as if they were miniature missiles.

The tailpipe emanated a billowing smoke screen while the truck fishtailed through the parking lot.

An intermittent popping noise, similar to the sound of fireworks, was heard over the roar of the truck's engine.

Trey assumed gunshots were fired at him, but he was unscathed and unaware of any bullets penetrating the truck.

As Trey steered the truck onto Nebraska Avenue, adrenaline and raw emotion raged through his body, ensuring that his right foot was pressed on the gas pedal with such force to put a hole through the floorboard.

Trey looked into his rearview mirror, relieved he did not see anyone in hot pursuit. However, in an abundance of caution, he turned onto a secondary road to be as obscure as possible.

Although Trey had escaped, he was riddled with guilt. His interaction with Cyn was the impetus for Mad Dog's jealous rage. Moreover, Trey left Cyn to face Mad Dog's wrath.

"What sort of punishment will Cyn be subjected to?" Trey asked himself. He cringed, envisioning Mad Dog throwing Cyn around like a rag doll.

At that moment, Trey was willing to put himself in harm's way to rescue Cyn. Without hesitation, he made a U-turn, steering his truck toward the Library Lounge. Trey drove past the Lounge parking lot as inconspicuously as possible. Not seeing anyone outside the bar, he parked on the periphery of the lot.

It was 1:45 am and all bars were required to close at 2 pm. Trey decided to wait for Mad Dog and Cyn to exit the bar. Trey watched as patrons, one by one, exited the bar and walked to their vehicles.

There was only one other vehicle in the parking lot. It was a 1960s International Scout. There were no doors or roofs. Mad Dog had severed the roof from the vehicle because he wanted a convertible.

But technically, removing the roof from the vehicle did not make it a convertible. There was no convertible top that went up and down. The vehicle was permanently sans roof.

If Trey were a betting man, Mad Dog, and Cyn would be next to emerge from the lounge. Within minutes, they were in plain sight. Mad Dog had his arm around Cyn's shoulder as if it were a death grip while her body awkwardly leaned toward him.

While Mad Dog and Cyn approached the Scout, Trey clicked on his truck's high beam lights, shifted the vehicle into drive, and descended upon them within moments.

As the high beams temporarily blinded Mad Dog, Trey yelled, "Cyn, get in the truck. Get in the truck, now."

Mad Dog's grip on her had lessened. She twisted and squirmed, escaping from his clenched hands, and made a run for it. Trey opened the passenger door on his truck and Cyn leaped in the front seat.

As Trey accelerated, he reached over to lock the passenger door, nearly losing control of the vehicle as Mad Dog made a lunging-desperate attempt to open the door.

Trey and Cyn shuddered as Mad Dog screeched, "Death to both of you."

Although Trey had rescued Cyn, he had placed her in great peril too.

There was no doubt Mad Dog would be coming for her.

As Trey remained contemplatively silent while motoring the truck on an isolated road toward downtown, he waited for Cyn's haranguing.

On cue, Cyn launched into her diatribe: "I thought my dreadful life could not be any worse," she said. "But then you appear out of nowhere to help me and now I will be captured dead or alive.

"At least I had a life before you came between me and Mad Dog," she said as her voice crescendoed into a fevered-angry pitch.

Trey pulled the truck onto the road, shifted it into park, and hung his head in despair.

He then said, "So you want me to take you back to him?"

Cyn faced Trey, looked at him squarely in the eyes, and nodded her head.

"It is the only chance we have," she said. "If I do not go back to him, he'll hunt us both down like a pack of wolves preying for their next meal."

Trey said nothing. The silence was his way of acquiescing.

"With any luck, I'll be home before him," she said, managing a faint grin to put a good face on her plan to return to Mad Dog.

What she did not want to do is cry. As Trey parked in a convenience store parking lot a stone's throw from her apartment, she exited the truck. Trey stared at her as she walked into the dark of the night.

Trey patrolled the area, vigilantly looking for the likes of Mad Dog. In his fury, he would end Mad Dog's life to save Cyn.

But a moment later, Trey told himself he was not a hitman.

Coming to his senses, Trey communicated to Cyn via a text message: "You need to call the police and request a protective order."

But Cyn refused to consider a legal solution, promptly following up with another text: "A few days of jail time and a protective order will not stop Mad Dog. You are the only one I can trust. You can end my suffering by putting an end to Mad Dog."

After reading the text, Trey exhaled, realizing he was smack in the middle of a precarious conundrum. He was damned if he did and damned if he did not. He wanted to be the crusader who protected people against abuse.

But now Trey had to face the very real possibility that his actions may lead to Mad Dog beating Cyn or killing her. Trey knew standing by idly was not an option. He had to do something. Anything less would be unacceptable.

Trey did his best thinking when driving. He drove along Nebraska Avenue for hours, contemplating his next move.

By this time, the sun was rising. Trey parked at a strip mall, sleeping for a few hours.

When Trey awakened by late morning, he drove to the Library Lounge, looking for Mad Dog.

The thought was not lost on him that the moment of truth had arrived for him. It was now or never. With that thought, Trey exited his truck and walked to the front door, realizing the optics of the situation did not bode well for him.

As he opened the door, Cyn instantly saw Trey and screamed, "There he is Trey!"

If there were any opportunities for Trey to have the upper hand of surprise, it had dissipated.

Trey knew his predicament was worsening by the moment. Mad Dog appeared surprised at how Cyn had responded upon Trey's arrival.

In a rare moment of melancholy, Mad Dog looked at Cyn and asked, "What in the hell are you doing?"

Cyn, placing her hands on hips in a defiant manner, responded, "Don't play all innocent with me, you S.O.B."

Mad Dog countered, "Not that I need to convince you or anyone else here, but this is pure fantasy. I have not laid a hand on you."

If Trey were ambivalent about his next move, he was further confused. Cyn's demonstrable words appeared to be contrived, whereas Mad Dog's response appeared to be sincere.

Cyn could see confusion in Treys' eyes and pivoted with her next move. She sauntered over to Trey, and removed sunglasses from her face, exposing her battered black and blue eyes. It was difficult for Trey to look at her. She was nearly unrecognizable with her discolored and swollen-disconfigured face.

As Trey stood spellbound, Cyn leaned into him and whispered, "You are the only one who can save me from him. It is either me or him."

If Trey did not previously know he was in an imbroglio, he did now. Cyn then stepped away from Trey and asked, "What are you going to do?"

Mad Dog was a high school dropout but was street-smart. Although he had not heard Cyn's whispers, he was reasonably certain she cast blame on him for her battered face.

Trey was in no position to determine whether Mad Dog was reprehensible for Cyn's facial wounds, but emotions were fueling his behavior. He turned toward Mad Dog and began to approach him. Mad Dog was not about to plead his innocence at this point. This was about defending himself against an outsider.

Trey felt as if Mad Dog's dark piercing eyes were staring through him. He then scoffed at Trey in disgust while uttering: "Where do you get off attempting to determine what I did or did not do to Cyn? You are not the law. All of us know what you are," MadDog said as his gravel voice trailed off.

Mad Dog then added: "You believe Cyn as if she is some sort of damsel in distress. What you don't realize little punk boy is she has you wrapped in the palm of her hand."

Trey came to his senses. Mad Dog, while crude, was making sense. Trey had allowed his emotions and feelings to cloud his judgment. He did not know Cyn and realized she could be lying through her teeth.

Trey asked himself whether Cyn had woven a tight web of deceit.

"Was Cyn besotted with Trey or just manipulating him as a pawn in a three-dimensional chess game?" Trey asked himself.

Mad Dog was trying to break Trey. He was convinced that if he were to make an aggressive move, Trey would depart the Lounge like a scared little boy.

Mad Dog picked up a half-filled Bud Light, finished it off, and then broke the bottle on the table. He then made an awkward lunge at Trey with the bottle in hand. As Mad Dog stumbled, he raised the bottle in an attempt to strike Trey. The bottle grazed Trey's face, As blood was running down his face, Cyn screamed, "Kill him, kill him."

At no time did Cyn come to the aid of Trey. Trey was not sure whom Cyn wanted to be killed. Regardless, it was a strange comment under the circumstances. But her statement did raise the specter of Cyn's intent.

Did she want Trey to do her dirty work by killing Mad Dog? Or, did she want Mad Dog to kill him? The latter question shook Trey to his core.

"What in God's name am I doing here?" Trey asked himself. He further mused, "I have placed myself smack-middle in a domestic dispute in which it is damn near impossible to determine the perpetrator and victim."

Trey was coming to his senses while standing on the bar floor while blood oozed from his chin. He was neither trained in law enforcement nor counseling. He candidly acknowledged to himself that his actions had exacerbated matters between Mad Dog and Cyn.

Trey pivoted to face Mad Dog. He then extended his hand and did his best mea culpa: "I have no business coming between you and Cyn."

At that moment, Mad Dog opened his balled fist and reciprocated with a handshake. Then Trey added, "I hope you and Cyn can patch things up."

Mad Dog responded, "Are you kidding me?" She was trying to use you to kill me. I am done with her."

Trey nodded as if Mad Dog had confirmed his worst fears. Trey looked downward, noticing his blood on the floor.

"I need to get to the emergency room before I lose any more blood," Trey said, trying to sound matter of factly.

Without hesitation, Mad Dog said he would drive Trey to the hospital. Mad Dog's outreach to Trey appeared to signal their confrontation had descended from an apotheosis.

But as the two men began walking to the door, one of the patrons shouted, "Watch out, she has a knife.

At that moment, both Trey and Mad Dog turned around. Cyn was wielding a switchblade that ripped Mad Dog's shirt and scraped along his chest. Cyn then attempted to go for the kill as she held the knife like a dagger and attempted to shove it into Mad Dog's midsection.

Trey stepped in, placing his hand around the knife, which severely cut his hand. Several patrons grabbed Cyn, wrestling her to the floor as her voice cried out in a blood-curdling scream.

Trey removed his shirt from his body and wrapped it around his hand. Mad Dog bear hugged Trey, then said, "Let's get you to the hospital before you bleed out."

Chapter 16

A Brighter Future

Mad Dog and Trey arrived at St. Petersburg General Hospital. Ironically, 18 months nearly had passed since Trey was at the same hospital on the cusp of death. But the optics were different this time.

Trey's involvement in a domestic dispute between Mad Dog and Cyn was not only foolish, but high risk and low reward. He knew his parents would be indignant, justifiably so.

After Trey had attempted to take his life, there was sensitivity and compassion for him to overcome the trials and tribulations in his young life. But Trey had no empathy for himself and did not expect anyone, especially Thomas and Katharine, to be a shoulder for him to cry on.

Trey received a blood transfusion and had stitched a facial cut on his cheekbone and a deep abrasion on the palm of his right hand. He asked if there would be permanent scarring.

The tending physician, Dr. Andrew Gottlieb, said he would not know for sure until the stitches were extracted, but suggested there may be permanent scarring.

"We can cross that bridge when we come to it," Dr. Gottlieb said. "Plastic surgery is an option."

Trey's thoughts immediately drifted to the movie, "Vanilla Sky," which featured Tom Cruise's character suffering a tormented life after his face was disfigured in an automobile accident.

Trey took a deep breath and mumbled to himself, "Hopefully I will not be a freak show."

He realized the hyperbole as his mind processed that thought.

Trey wanted to be released from the hospital, but Dr. Gottlieb insisted he not drive following the blood transfusion.

Trey did not want to contact his parents. He was hoping to insulate himself from a scathing rebuke from them.

As Trey contemplated his next move, a medical assistant informed him a man at the nurse station had offered to take him home.

"This is an offer I can't refuse," Trey told himself. He signed release forms before eagerly joining Mad Dog. Trey thanked Mad Dog profusely, which prompted Mad Dog to respond:

"You are welcome, Trey, but if you thank me one more time, I ain't giving you a ride home."

As Trey hopped into Mad Dog's 1972 Lincoln Continental, his cell phone was buzzing incessantly with text messages. Thomas and Katharine had sent a dozen text messages to Trey's phone. Katharine sent the first message at 7:30 pm when she delivered dinner to Trey's apartment. She followed up to no avail over the next three hours.

After Thomas arrived at Trey's apartment at 11 pm, he too initiated several text messages over the ensuing hours. Trey had failed to answer a single message, which put his parents on high alert.

Like many parents, Thomas and Katharine fed off their fears and paranoia. They had talked themselves into believing Trey was in great peril. The previous night, they had contacted the St. Petersburg Police Department.

Thomas and Katharine provided the police department with a description of Trey and his truck. Dispatch advised patrol officers to look for Trey's vehicle.

But Thomas and Katharine were told they could not file a missing person's report until 24 hours had passed since Trey was last seen.

Trey opted not to call his parents. Instead, he sent a text, attempting to assure them he is ok. Despite Trey's assurances, Thomas and Katharine were not placated.

Thomas' concerns were pragmatic. He wondered how Trey functioned in his job if his days were turning into nights and vice versa.

It should not have been surprising Thomas and Katharine were hell-bent on returning to Trey's apartment to evaluate their son's well-being.

For Trey and other Gen Zs who no longer reside in their parents' home, a late-night visit from Thomas and Katharine would be persona non grata.

But any mother and father would implicitly understand Thomas and Katharine's decision to check on their son in the wee hours of the morning. This understanding is consistent with parents' love for their children throughout life.

That sentiment was poignantly illustrated in the 1989 movie, Parenthood, when Jason Robards' character tells his adult son, Steve Martin, that parenthood is not like crossing the goal line and spiking the ball as if there is a finality for parenting.

"Once a parent, always a parent," Robards tells Martin at the end of the scene.

Meanwhile, Thomas and Katharine were heading to Trey's apartment with great celerity until they were forced to find an all-night gas station open.

Thomas had a proclivity to cap his fuel costs at five dollars per stop. It was not as if gas were 50 cents a gallon when five dollars would nearly top off the fuel tank. This was in 2019 when five dollars would pay for two gallons of gas.

The gas stop drew the ire of Katharine, especially in light of Trey's dubious history of attempted suicide and now, unknown whereabouts.

"Damn you, Thomas," Katharine said in utter frustration. "You are going to give me a nervous breakdown with your penne ante purchases."

They arrived as Trey and Mad Dog entered the driveway.

As Trey approached his parents, he cordially uttered, "Hey Mom and Dad, what are you doing here?"

Thomas and Katharine paused. Then Thomas sent a strong non-verbal message by staring at his watch.

It read 5:45 am. No words were exchanged as Thomas and Katharine glared at Trey.

Their gaze was redirected from Trey to Mad Dog The awkward silence was broken when Thomas asked Trey to introduce his friend.

"Mom and Dad, this is Mad Dog," Trey said, instantly cringing and immediately presuming Thomas and Katharine would not embrace a friend with that moniker.

Mad Dog attempted to alleviate damage control:

"Nice to meet each of you, Mr. and Mrs. Barry. My name is Patrick John."

As far as Trey was concerned, the name—Mad Dog—was immaterial.

But as Thomas and Katharine observed Patrick John, they not only were unimpressed with his nickname but his speech too. He spoke in slang and broken English, confirming his lack of education.

The more Thomas heard from Trey's new friend, the more incensed he became. Thomas' oft-repeated advice for Trey was people are judged by the friends they keep.

Trey knew Patrick John's intellect was higher functioning than his verbal articulation.

Trey responded with a somewhat esoteric plea:

"Please don't judge a book by its cover."

Trey beseeched his father to look beyond the superficial qualities of Patrick John.

"If it were not for Patrick John, I would not be here," Trey said. "He saved my life."

"At his core, he is a good man," Trey added. I am asking each of you, Dad and Mom, to be open-minded and allow him to demonstrate the person he is."

Thomas acknowledged his frustration should be directed at Trey, not Patrick John.

"Trey, your mother and I suffered along with you after your near-death experience," Thomas said, not comfortable, even at this point, to utter the words of attempted suicide. "But with a second chance at life, you obviously are placing yourself at-risk and in doing so, insensitively tormenting your parents."

Trey drooped his shoulders and hung his head. He knew Thomas was right.

Trey had been fixated on helping victims of bullying. For him, that need superseded everything else.

Trey's first course of business was to discontinue vigilantism. Once again, he would have to reboot his life.

Trey approached Thomas and Katharine and offered the following afterthought: "I apologize for my lack of empathy and for putting each of you through another hellish experience due to my actions."

Katharine tearfully reached out to Trey as mother and son embraced. Trey then extended his hand to Thomas, They hardly shook hands as Thomas said:

"At this late hour, each of us needs a few hours of rest. Your mother and I are going to head home, but please call us later this afternoon."

Thomas then turned to Patrick John, gesturing to him to accompany Trey.

Patrick John nodded in appreciation for the invitation.

After a few hours of sleep, Trey contacted his father. Thomas said he would like to discuss a proposal over dinner.

Trey was convinced he would have to accept an offer in order not to further alienate himself from his parents. The fact he did not know the terms of the offer did not seem to matter.

Trey and Patrick John made a concerted effort to arrive a few minutes before the dinner hour. One of Thomas' pet peeves was tardiness. The last thing Trey wanted to do is create negative mojo before dinner and the impending offer, whatever it is.

Aidan greeted Thomas and Patrick John at the front door.

"Dad is on the back porch, grilling steaks," she said, adding, "I don't know what is going on, but he wants to have a word with you."

Trey knew Thomas was incapable of merely stating a few words in conversation with anyone. The longstanding joke in the Barry family was Thomas' inability for brevity.

To say that Thomas had the Irish gift for gab was an understatement. He was reputed as loquacious. And, he always had to have the last word.

Trey and Patrick John made a beeline for the back porch. Thomas, the gracious host, extended a robust handshake to each of them.

"Thanks for coming over, Trey and Patrick John," Thomas said.

Patrick John politely responded, "Mr. Barry, you can call me P.J. if you would like." Thomas nodded affably and said, "So P.J. it is."

Thomas gestured for Trey and PJ to pluck a beer from the 45-quart Yeti cooler on the porch.

After Trey and PJ popped the tops of their beers, Thomas launched into an offer for their consideration:

"I've purchased a little land in Pinellas Park. It is more like a field."

Trey and PJ quizzically looked at one another as if to ask where Thomas is going with this discussion. Then in Thomas' next breath, he clarified how an empty field pertained to Trey and PJ.

"I have been cobbling together a few dollars here and there for a business on the side," Thomas said as he pulled on his right ear lobe. "The garage will be built on the premises for boats in need of fiberglass and wood repair."

Thomas said his newfound business will be the "Boat Doctor."

"I like that," PJ said, his voice amplified in excitement.

Trey was reserved, asking his dad whether he was skilled in the art of boat repair.

"It always has been a passion of mine, but I've never had the financial wherewithal and time until now to make a go of it," Thomas said. "I'd like to retire from my day job and delve into this in a couple of years."

Trey looked confused, then asked, "So dad, how do you get this business up and running if you can't devote much time to it now?"

Thomas smiled, knowing Trey's question was the perfect segue to make his offer.

"That is where you and PJ come in," Thomas said. "I will pay tuition for each of you to complete a series of career technical courses in boat repair over the next year."

PJ could not contain his excitement as he smiled from ear to ear while looking at Trey for affirmation.

Trey, like his father, had a passion for boats. Trey began to nod his head.

But before Trey verbally responded to the offer, Thomas added a wrinkle, "I already have a few suitors, one of whom is the owner of a wooden lapstrake Albury runabout. She is a classic, but needs the stringers and deck repaired."

Trey had a special affinity for classic vessels with traditional lines and contour. He could no longer contain his enthusiasm.

P.J. did not have to say a word. His expression with his mouth agape in awe of the proposal manifested his response. He was overcome with gratitude and what he considered an opportunity of a lifetime.

Trey expressed gratitude: "Dad, this is a dream come true and an offer we can't refuse. Thank you."

Thomas beamed with happiness. He could not remember the last time he felt so good, so good about anything.

"So," Thomas said, basking in the moment, explained his version of a quid pro quo:

"I will pay tuition for each of you to earn passing grades and complete the coursework in each of the next two semesters," Thomas said.

When Trey and P.J. were not attending class and studying, they were expected to assist in the construction of the new facility.

Trey and PJ accepted Thomas' offer not knowing they would earn $12 an hour and receive a modest bonus when they completed their coursework.

"Just one other thing," Thomas said. "The work day will begin at 6 am."

The early morning work schedule was intentional.

As Thomas later explained to Katharine, "We can't impose a curfew on young men who live independently from us. But hopefully, a strictly imposed work schedule will ensure their days are for school and work and the nights are to sleep well."

Katharine asked how she and Thomas could afford to place Trey and P.J. on the payroll and pay for their tuition. Thomas repositioned himself and cleared his throat:

"We can liquidate a couple of our IRAs for immediate cash over the short term," he said.

Thomas acknowledged withdrawal penalties from their IRAs. But the fees, he said, pale in comparison to what can be achieved for Trey and PJ.

Katharine, reputed as somewhat of a penny pincher, nodded in agreement, then added:

"We can do this for the short term, but if the boat repair business does not make money at some point, I am afraid this effort, as altruistically motivated as it is, will eventually be doomed."

Thomas appeared as if he were a stratagem extraordinaire, or so it would seem, with purchasing the lot, building a facility, soliciting customers, and offering jobs and a much-needed direction for Trey and PJ.

In truth, Thomas was moved by his gut to segue into retirement with the boat-renovation business. His ambling proved to be good timing to offer jobs for two men who desperately needed employment and for Thomas who could not run the business alone.

It was a synergy of sorts. But more importantly, Thomas, step by step, created a blueprint for Trey and PJ to redefine themselves with the stability that comes with gainful employment.

Trey had a predilection for boat design. He studied the lines and contours of classic vessels, from a genre of DownEast hulls to iconic deep-V Hunt and Bertram designs, to the Bahamian configuration of Albury boats.

Trey spoke about boats as if they had a human quality, referring to them as the feminine gender. People who questioned Trey's maritime nomenclature could be forgiven if they did not know the storied tradition of sailors referring to their ships in female-laced pronouns.

Moreover, maritime history suggests that most vessels were named after women. It was not uncommon for sailing vessels in the 18th and 19th centuries to manifest female figurines on the bowsprit.

Even pirate ships were named after women. Black Beard's flagship was none other than Queen Ann's Revenge.

P.J. was not a maritime aficionado, but he wanted to be adroit at something, anything. He had, however, enjoyed carpentry, especially constructing wooden furniture in shop class during middle school. He embraced the opportunity to renovate boats, especially the wooden variety. He intuitively knew this would be the turning point in his life.

P.J. and Trey were in the same bailiwick: jack of all trades and master of none. This would be their crossroads: making good on this opportunity would bode well for their quality of life. Failing to do so would retrograde them into their former lives.

If the latter were to be P.J.'s plight, it would most likely be his death knell.

For P.J., there would be no returning from the world of debauchery and reprobates. PJ had no lost love for his former life and those associated with it. He was not about to waste this opportunity.

Trey took pride in his craft but understood recompense—receiving a fair and reasonable fee for a job well done.

As Trey's former clinical psychologist, Gerald, had hoped, Trey was mentally and emotionally balancing the respect and dignity of others with self-assertiveness. The most notable example of this is how he responded to unruly customers.

At Thomas' behest, Trey photographed every step in boat-restoration projects. The photographs served to document the actual work and to provide customers with images of how boats looked before and after restoration. One customer who had obtained his boat a day earlier, burst through the front door of the shop as Trey was preparing to close. The customer, a middle-aged man with a foul mouth, clearly wanted to be heard. He slammed the door to ensure Trey was aware of his presence and rang the service bell on the front counter and then gruffly barked, "Anyone work around this damn place?"

Within moments, Trey appeared, politely responding, "Is there anything I can do for you, Dell?"

"You're damn right," Dell said, annunciating each word to emphasize his anger. 'You guys charged me for quality craftsmanship when in fact the work was shoddy and incomplete. Trey, maintaining his composure, asked Dell to elaborate.

"Why don't you look at my boat," Dell said. "It is outside. It speaks for itself." Within moments, Dell pointed to the keel of the boat. The outer coat of white gel coat had been chaffed.

"I paid you a pretty penny to gel coat the entire bottom of the boat and you do a half-ass, unfinished job," Dell said. "I want my money back."

Trey knew the bottom of the boat had been completely gel coated. He knew this because he had done the work himself and had the pictures to prove it. Internally, Trey was intimidated. Victimized by bullies will do that. However, externally, Trey stood his ground.

"I can't do that, sir," Trey said, responding to Dell's demand for reimbursement. 'When you picked up the boat last evening, the keel did not look like this.

"Something happened to the keel after you picked up the boat," Trey said.

Dell responded in typical fashion as a rude customer rocked back on his heels: "You calling me a liar, son?"

Trey deftly did not answer Dell's question. Instead, he reached for the scrapbook of the pictures depicting the boat as a finished project.

"As you can see, sir, the keel was gel-coated with wax and shine when you retrieved it," Trey said.

Dell suddenly was at a loss for words. He turned on his heels without the slightest regret. As Dell exited the shop, Trey reflected that such customers never apologize because they are jackasses at their core. He smiled at that thought and then pondered with self-adulation that he had become a different man. He knew the old Trey would have been brow-beaten into Dell's Rambo-type tactics.

As Trey headed home, Thomas and Katharine contacted him via cell phone.

"We have a little surprise for you," Thomas said. "I'll let your mother explain."

Katharine told her son not to make plans for the upcoming Independence Day weekend. "We would like you and P.J. to accompany us to the Jimmy Buffett concert on Biscayne Bay in Miami."

Epilogue

Trey was stoked about attending the Buffett Concert. He had grown up listening to music of his parents' generation. Soundtracks from Jimmy Buffett and the Coral Reef Band were his favorites. The genre of music, a mix of Calypso and Western, allowed him to mentally and emotionally escape into the tropical paradise of a beachcomber's life.

As an adolescent, Trey often fell asleep to the tunes of Changes in Latitude, Changes in Altitude, The Son of a Son of a Sailor, A School Boy's Heart, and his personal favorite, Bob Roberts Society Band.

On the day of the concert, Thomas, Katharine, Trey, Aidan, Brendan, Finn, and PJ packed into the Barry family van to head south. The Barrys wanted to arrive early so they could park at LaSalle Catholic High School, overlooking Biscayne Bay and juxtaposed to an Ampla Theatre where the concert would be held.

Upon arrival, Katharine quickly exited the van, saying she would return as soon as possible. About 30 minutes later, Katharine approached the van with another woman. Thomas, Finn, Aidan, Brendan, and PJ were beaming.

All but Trey knew who the other woman was none other than Mallory.

"The concert is not the only surprise," Katharine said. Trey stood as if he were mesmerized. Mallory, in a low-cut red dress, sashayed her way to Trey, opening her arms for an embrace. The two hugged and laughed.

They were the same people at their very core, yet they were different too.

Mallory intuitively sensed Trey had a newfound confidence in him. In past years, Trey could not hold eye contact when she looked at him with her piercing brown eyes.

But now, Trey was looking into her eyes as if time were standing still. And, Mallory had appeared to have recovered physically and emotionally from the hellish evening in which they were publicly humiliated.

Mallory's dark maim had grown back, as well as her eyebrows. As far as Trey was concerned, she was more attractive than ever. She no longer was a victim. Her self-confidence returned as she smiled and met Trey's gaze.

Truth be known, Trey and Mallory had feelings for one another, but parted ways because their interactions reminded them of their living nightmare.

At this moment, Trey and Mallory's interlude was temporarily placed on hold as Katharine tapped them on their shoulders with the pronouncement:

"Ok love birds, let's inflate the rafts and tubes for the concert."

Thomas and Katharine had seemingly thought of everything for the concert, including a compressor to inflate the flotation devices. As Jimmy Buffett and the Coral Reef Band were practically at the water's edge, the Barry family, PJ, and Mallory were floating on Biscayne Bay with cold ones in hand among hundreds of others as the music blared through the ocean breeze.

Life was grand. Trey uncharacteristically was uninhibited. He crooned lyrics, drank beer and even awkwardly fell into the water attempting to kiss Mallory as they were side by side on their floating tubes.

Trey laughed and Mallory smiled. She was not bothered by Trey's social awkwardness and clumsiness. She knew he was a good soul to his core and his character was beyond reproach.

Trey was at the apex of his happiness. His school-boy effervescence prompted him to swim to his father's unoccupied paddle board, climb atop it, and cannonball into the water.

But for Trey, the best was yet to come. After a short break, Jimmy Buffett announced he had a special request to play Bob Robert's Society Band.

As an adolescent, Trey occasionally lapsed into sleep listening to this song, which was a melodic combination of Calypso drums and the big band music of the 1940s.

"This one is for you, Trey," Jimmy Buffett crooned: "...It's the Bob Roberts Society Band. Playing every Sunday at the Orange Grove Stand. They don't play brunch and they don't play loud. It's the magic of the music that still draws a crowd..."

As the number ended, Trey asked, somewhat bewildered to no one in particular, "How did this happen?"

Katharine nodded in the direction of Thomas.

"Your father knows somebody who knows somebody who knows Jimmy," Katharine said, giggling like a schoolgirl.

As the concert drew to a close, concertgoers made a mad dash, paddling to a nearby landing.

But Trey and Mallory basked in the late-afternoon sunshine, soaking up every moment to fully appreciate a glorious day like no other.

Trey and Mallory, side by side, held one another's hand and were transfixed in a chilled mindset as if they were living a dream.

Then Trey broke the silence.

"I know you feel what I do. This is a new beginning for both of us. Let's avoid a long-distance relationship."

Trey's voice went silent, but Mallory could have finished his thought. She intuitively knew Trey was implying they are survivors of a horrific past in which they deserve an opportunity to grow together in a relationship without the challenges of living apart.

Mallory squeezed his hand as an affirmation of his sentiments. She smiled, looking at him, then said, "I would like that, but it will take time. I need to return to Tallahassee to complete my final semester."

"You could live with us," Trey impulsively responded before processing concerns over morality and not consulting with PJ.

"Trey, cohabitation is a non-starter," Mallory said, a devout Catholic. "Besides, my dad would kill me and then you."

Trey nervously laughed. Mallory's comments were not exactly the response he was looking for, but he respected her for taking the moral high road.

They walked to Mallory's car, then embraced. Mallory fidgeted with her car keys. At that moment, he looked into her eyes, placed his hands on her shoulders, and softly said, "I am not going to say goodbye because we will see one another soon. "You are my kindred spirit and soul mate."

Trey stopped short of conveying his love for her, but Trey's love for Mallory was unmistakably clear.

Mallory nodded, adding "Me too," intimating the same feelings Trey had for her. He could see the sincerity in her eyes.

Mallory then asked for Trey's indulgence.

Trey paused, waiting to hear her request.

"I will be visiting my parents next month and would like you to join me."

Trey instantly recollected her father's dismissive treatment of him.

But he knew delving into that interaction would be hurtful for Mallory. Managing to flash a smile, Trey said, "I would be pleased to join you and your parents."

Trey had given Mallory the perfect response. She blew him a kiss and turned the ignition in her Mini Cooper, making her way toward the I-95 northbound ramp for Tallahassee. She extended her hand from the driver's window, waving goodbye. Trey reciprocated.

In the immediate days that followed, Thomas and Katharine were concerned Trey might sink into the throes of depression if his budding relationship with Mallory were to sour.

But that's what parents do: worry about their children. Mallory had given them no reason to believe her relationship with Trey was anything but stable. Their love for one another was not merely besotted. They knew one another beyond the superficial pretentiousness of romance. She and Trey were relying on the power of prayer and their faith in God to overcome their loving-distance relationship.

And, their faith as practicing Catholics gave them an imbued confidence that as a couple, they would persevere through life's challenges with rooted unconditional love for one another.

Trey no longer held contempt for parents whose children were bullies. He understood there are reasons beyond parenting to explain incorrigible behavior.

Trey, no longer a naïve unabashed optimist, had become a confident-resilient survivor.

Trey realized he was not better than anyone else, but no one else was better than him. He was convinced with the coping strategies and tools he had gleaned from Gerald and Fr. Liam, coupled with his inner circle of Thomas, Katharine, Aidan, Brendan, Finn, PJ and now Mallory, he was ready to embark on the rest of his life with unbridled resolve.

Trey had acquired a sense of assertiveness and had grown in his spirituality, having a deeper appreciation for his faith and God's countless blessings that had been bestowed upon him.

He reminded himself daily of the scripture quoted in Matthew 17:20, which he kept in his billfold for safekeeping: "If you have faith the size of a mustard seed, you can move mountains."

Trey's mental health was sufficiently stable that he embraced the famous quote – "Be not afraid" – from Pope John Paul II. The quote became the pontiff's rallying cry in his rousing exhortation for God's people, particularly the young, to be unafraid in overcoming life's challenges.

From the ashes of despair, Trey had been reborn. He had become a realist, adjusting his proverbial sails to address the changing winds of life. He was neither the optimist who would expect the winds to favorably change nor the pessimist who would complain about the unfavorable winds.

This was not to suggest Trey was a completely healthy, whole individual. But who is? He had a healthy level of anger to stand his ground when need be. And, he had mercy in his heart to forgive those who trespass against him.

Contemplating mercy always reminded him of a famous quote from Abraham Lincoln: "Malice to none; charity for all." That quote rang in his ears as he walked along St. Pete Beach during a late afternoon. He occasionally stopped, picking up seashells one by one, flicking them as they skipped over the waves.

As the sun began to set over the Gulf of Mexico. he looked upward as if he were asking God whether it was time to plot a course for the rest of his life.

Trey had an abiding sense the time is now for him to chart what he deemed was his destiny. The storms Trey had weathered in his short life foretold him there would be choppy waters and an occasional tempest in his voyage of life.

Trey realized he would need to adjust metaphorical sails when the conditions demanded him to do so.

His painful life had prepared him for the worst, but he was hoping for the best, never forgetting the adage that rising tides lift all boats.

That thought, as it always did, induced a smile. As he looked at the horizon, he conspicuously opened his arms, uttering: "Here I am Lord. Thank you for the gift of life."

-- End --

www.ingramcontent.com/pod-product-compliance
Lightning Source LLC
LaVergne TN
LVHW041945070526
838199LV00051BA/2917